THE MATH KIDS: A SEQUENCE OF EVENTS

BOOK 2

THE MATH KIDS:
A SEQUENCE OF EVENTS

BY DAVID COLE
ILLUSTRATED BY SHANNON O'TOOLE

COMMON DEER PRESS
WWW.COMMONDEERPRESS.COM

Published by Common Deer Press Incorporated.

Published in 2018 by Common Deer Press
3203-1 Scott St.
Toronto, ON
M5V 1A1

This book is a work of fiction. Names, characters,
places, and incidents are either the product of the
author's imagination or are used fictitiously.

Library of Congress Cataloging-in-Publication Data
Cole, David.-First edition.
The Math Kids: A Sequence of Events / David Cole
ISBN: 978-1-988761-30-5 (print)
ISBN: 978-1-988761-31-2 (e-book)

Cover Image: © Shannon O'Toole
Book Design: Ellie Sipila
Printed in Canada

WWW.COMMONDEERPRESS.COM

FOR MARY ANNE, WHO ALWAYS
MADE SURE I HAD PLENTY OF
BOOKS TO READ.

CHAPTER I

I ronically, it had all started with a math puzzle. The next thing I knew, the newest member of our math club had disappeared.

After three days without a sign of her, we decided it was time for the Math Kids to do something about it.

But I'm getting ahead of myself, so I'll begin at the beginning...

It was Friday, and we had almost made it through another week with Mrs. Gouche. She was our fourth-grade teacher and wasn't too bad most of the time. I liked that she had separate math groups, so we didn't get stuck doing the easy math with Robbie Colson and Sniffy Brown.

Sniffy's real name is Brian, but everyone calls him Sniffy because he always has a runny nose and sniffs loudly. We never call him Sniffy to his face, of course. He is friends with Robbie, Bill Cape, and Bryce Bookerman, the class bullies.

"Don't forget that we have Math Kids club tomorrow,"

I reminded Stephanie on the way into class. I'm the president of the Math Kids club at McNair Elementary School. I hadn't exactly been elected to the position, though. Stephanie Lewis had said I should be president since the club was my idea, and Justin Grant, my best friend since kindergarten, hadn't objected. There was no need for an election because there were only three of us in the club.

I already knew Justin was coming to the meeting because we had talked about possible problems to tackle while we walked to school that morning. Justin had a new book of math puzzles he was planning to bring.

You're probably thinking that all we do in the Math Kids club is sit around and solve math problems. That was how the club had started, but it sure took a few strange turns along the way. Who would have thought we could use math to crack a case the police couldn't solve? Still, the original idea for the club was to solve math problems. And when all the excitement with the burglars was over, trust me, that's all we wanted to do.

"Wouldn't miss it, Jordan!" Stephanie said. "No, wait! I have soccer practice, so it would have to be after that."

I rolled my eyes as I took my seat in class. This would take some finessing on my part. Justin and Stephanie had had more than one blowup over her soccer practices colliding with our math club. But finding a way to avoid another shouting match was a problem I'd face after school.

Mrs. Gouche has been giving our math group

tougher and tougher problems as the school year goes on. She knows that Stephanie, Justin, and I are good at math and really like hard problems, so she has made it her mission to challenge us. This day's problem, for example, was no exception.

"This, my friends, is called The Sixes Problem. Catherine, can you hand this to Jordan?"

The girl who sat in front of me—Catherine... something—handed me the problem sheet. I noticed she took a long look at it before passing it back to me.

I smiled, knowing that she probably wouldn't have the first clue about how to solve the kind of problems our teacher had been giving us. Little did I know that she actually knew a lot more than I thought and would end up being right in the middle of our next mystery.

Mrs. Gouche put her dry-erase marker down and returned to her desk. She had an evil glint in her eye and my heart started to beat a little faster.

The problem *looked* simple enough when I first scanned it. We had to use three of the same number, like 2, 2, 2 or 5, 5, 5, and any mathematical operations, like multiplication, division, or addition, to make 6. For example, to solve for the number 2 we could use $2 \times 2 + 2 = 6$. It didn't look difficult, but it turned out to be much tougher than we thought!

WAIT! DO YOU WANT TO TRY TO SOLVE THIS PUZZLE BEFORE SEEING IF THE MATH KIDS CAN DO IT? FOR EACH NUMBER FROM 0 TO 9, USE THREE OF THE SAME NUMBER AND ANY MATHEMATICAL OPERATIONS TO MAKE THE NUMBER 6. FOR EXAMPLE, FOR THE NUMBER 2, ANOTHER POSSIBLE SOLUTION IS $2 + 2 + 2 = 6$. GOOD LUCK!

We went to the whiteboard and started working. We easily came up with answers for the numbers 2 and 6:

$2 \times 2 + 2 = 6$

$6 + 6 - 6 = 6$

The problem was that we had to do the same thing with all the numbers from 0 to 9.

While the rest of the class was working on their social studies homework, the three of us stood at the whiteboard, dry-erase markers in our hands, as we tried to solve for all the numbers.

Justin got us the next two answers when he remembered that any number divided by itself is just one.

That means that $5 \div 5$ is just 1 so we could use $5 + 5 \div 5 = 6$. We used the same trick to solve for the number 7.

That meant we had four down and six to go:

0)
1)
2) $2 + 2 + 2 = 6$
3)
4)
5) $5 + (5 \div 5) = 6$
6) $6 + (6 - 6) = 6$
7) $7 - (7 \div 7) = 6$
8)
9)

Zero and one looked impossible. We thought they might really be impossible, too. We had lost a class pizza party when Stephanie bet Mrs. Gouche that we would solve a problem called the Bridges of Königsberg. It turned out that the problem didn't have an answer. Score one for Mrs. Gouche!

"I don't think there are answers for zero and one," Justin complained.

"Me neither," I added. "Let's work on three and four. I'm sure we can get those."

Three turned out to be pretty easy: $(3 \times 3) - 3 = 6$. We were halfway there!

And halfway there was as far as we got. We stared at the board and made some attempts at new ideas, but the last five answers remained out of our reach.

The three o'clock dismissal bell rang while we were still staring at the board.

"We did pretty well, Mrs. Gouche," I announced. "We've only got three more to go."

She glanced up at the board.

"It looks like five more to go, Mr. Waters. Did you forget about zero and one?" she asked, turning her focus back to the papers she was grading.

"But those are impossible," I protested. "You were trying to trick us again."

"No tricks this time," she said. "There are answers for every number from zero to nine."

We stared at the remaining problems on the board. There was no way we could do anything to get three 1s to somehow equal 6. And the 0s? Forget about it.

The class started to gather up their papers and books and stuff them into backpacks. Robbie and his buddies pushed each other as they rushed to get out of the room. None of the bullies had detention for a change, so they were anxious to get out to the playground for a game of soccer.

We were on temporary good terms with the bullies. I wasn't sure how long it would last, but at least, for the moment, I didn't have to worry about them knocking my backpack to the floor, or tripping me as I walked past them, or threatening to rearrange my face at recess. We had Stephanie to thank for that. It had been her idea to have Robbie's dad help us catch the burglars. Mr. Colson is a police officer, but usually doesn't do anything more exciting than writing parking tickets. When we used our math skills to figure out when and where the burglars were going to hit next,

Stephanie had found a way for Mr. Colson to get credit for cracking the case. Robbie's dad was happy, which meant we were on Robbie's good side—temporarily anyway.

"Well, I guess I know what we'll be working on in the Math Kids club tomorrow," I said with a frown. Normally, I would have been happy to work on a tough math problem, but I knew there was no way we were going to be able to solve this one.

"Let's start early tomorrow," Justin said. "We could meet at—"

"I've got soccer practice," Stephanie interrupted.

"Of course you do," Justin replied sarcastically. "The sun is up, so you must have soccer practice."

Stephanie gave him an irritated look as she tugged on her ponytail. Wanting to avoid an argument, I jumped in quickly.

"How about Justin and I get started and you come over after practice?" I asked.

"Yeah, that would work," she said.

"It doesn't really matter," Justin sulked. "We're never going to get answers for zero and one anyway."

"Factorials," said a small voice near the door.

"What did you say?" asked Justin.

"Factorials," repeated the small voice, which we could now see had come out of the mouth of the girl who sat in front of me, Catherine...Duchesne. I knew I'd remember her last name eventually. "You need to use factorials to solve for zero and one."

"How is a factory going to help us solve a math problem?" I asked.

"Not a factory," she said, laughing. "Factorials."

And with that, she was out of the room and disappeared into the crowd of students headed down the hallway to the exits.

CHAPTER 2

I was halfway through my second bowl of cereal on Saturday morning when Justin called.

"Come on, we're going to practice," he said without even a hello.

"Practice what?"

"Soccer."

You could have knocked me over with a feather. Justin was not the most athletic kid. The only sport he kind of liked was basketball, which was kind of funny since he was the shortest kid in the class.

"Why are we going to practice soccer?" I asked.

"We're not. We're doing math," he replied. "I'll meet you out in front of your house in ten minutes."

I was completely confused, but I scarfed down the rest of my cereal and grabbed the pair of sneakers I had left by the front door. I was lacing them up on my front porch when Justin appeared. He was wearing his backpack, which looked even more stuffed than usual.

"Let's go," he called. "Time's a wasting."

I finished tying my shoes and followed Justin, who was already on his way down the street.

"Care to explain what we're doing?" I asked.

"It's simple. If we can't get Stephanie to come to math club in the morning because of her stupid soccer practice, we'll take the math club to her."

We got to the soccer park fifteen minutes later. There were six soccer fields filled with kids of all ages. It took a little while to find Stephanie's field, but we finally saw her doing a dribbling drill with her teammates. While I watched her practice (she was amazing—by far the fastest girl on her team and she handled the ball like it was on a string), Justin dug into his backpack. He pulled out a portable easel and extended the legs. Next came a mini whiteboard, then a set of colored markers. Finally, he pulled out a roll of cellophane tape and The Sixes Problem with our previous answers filled in. He taped the paper to the bottom of the whiteboard.

"There you go," he said with satisfaction. "A portable classroom."

The look on his face was so serious that I had to laugh. He looked crestfallen for a moment, then broke into his own grin.

"That's pretty low-tech for you, isn't it?" I asked, knowing that Justin loved computers and spent hours every day playing fast-paced video games.

"I couldn't find an extension cord long enough to make it to the soccer field." Justin smiled at his own joke.

"So how is Stephanie going to play soccer and do math at the same time?" I asked.

"They have to give her a break every once in a while, don't they?"

"Yeah, I guess."

"Well, she can do math while she rests."

Justin's plan ended up working very well. It turned out Stephanie could do fancy footwork and fancy brainwork at the same time. As she practiced throw-ins from the sideline, she called over to Justin.

"Can we use square roots?" she asked.

Her coach wasn't happy about the distraction, but her suggestion was genius.

A square root of a number is a value that, when multiplied by itself, gives the number. The square root of 4 (written as $\sqrt{4}$) is 2, for example, since $2 \times 2 = 4$. The square root of 9 is 3, since $3 \times 3 = 9$.

As soon as Stephanie got the words "square roots" out of her mouth, Justin was already writing an answer for the number 4 on the mini whiteboard:

$\sqrt{4} + \sqrt{4} + \sqrt{4} = 6$

Since $\sqrt{4} = 2$, it was just like saying $2 + 2 + 2 = 6$.

I got the next one myself:

$(9 + 9) \div \sqrt{9} = 6$

Justin turned his head to one side as he squinted at my answer. I knew that look, so I explained it to him.

"Nine plus nine equals eighteen and the square root of nine is three," I explained.

"So, it's just eighteen divided by three," he finished.

"Nice work, Stephanie!" I called out. "We got two more!"

She smiled and gave me a high five as she ran past. "Nice job, guys!" she shouted, earning another look of disapproval from her coach. A short time later, it was the coach giving Stephanie a high five as she found the upper corner of the goal with a difficult left-footed shot.

Justin solved the toughest part of The Sixes Problem yet when he came up with a solution using three 8s while Stephanie was on a water break. She and I had to stare at his answer for some time before we finally got it:

$$8 - \sqrt{(\sqrt{(8 + 8)})} = 6$$

Stephanie talked it out as she tried to figure out what Justin had done.

"So, eight plus eight equals sixteen," she started. "Then you take the square root of sixteen to get four."

That's when I got it.

"And then you take the square root of four to get two," I added, pointing at the second square root symbol.

"And eight minus two equals six," finished Justin. He was trying not to smile, but I could tell he was very proud of what he had come up with.

"That's brilliant!" shouted Stephanie, drawing another stern look from her coach.

"You want to get back in the game?" he called over.

"Gotta go. We should be done in a few minutes, though," she said as she hustled back out on the field. "See you back at your house, Justin."

Justin packed up his portable classroom. We had solved all but 0 and 1, which I was pretty sure were impossible, despite what Mrs. Gouche had told us.

$$2 + 2 + 2 = 6$$
$$(3 \times 3) - 3 = 6$$
$$\sqrt{4} + \sqrt{4} + \sqrt{4} = 6$$
$$5 + (5 \div 5) = 6$$
$$6 + (6 - 6) = 6$$
$$7 - (7 \div 7) = 6$$
$$8 - \sqrt{(\sqrt{(8 + 8)})} = 6$$
$$(9 + 9) \div \sqrt{9} = 6$$

A short while later, back at Justin's house, Stephanie

started the official Math Kids meeting with two questions.

"Who was that girl yesterday and what is a factorial?"

I could answer the first question. I was hoping Justin could answer the second.

"Her name is Catherine Duchesne," I told Stephanie. "She sits in front of me."

"Does she know anything about math?" she asked.

"How should I know?" I said. "I don't think I've ever even heard her speak before. I think she's in the red math group."

The math groups in our room were all named after colors. We were in the yellow group. After that came blue, then red, and then finally green: the group that Robbie and Sniffy and the rest of the bullies were in.

"How can someone in the red group know so much about math?" Stephanie asked. "I don't think that's possible."

"Well, in this case, it's definitely possible," Justin chimed in.

Stephanie and I looked at him.

"I asked my dad about factorials last night, and I think Catherine may be right," Justin said.

"Are you kidding me?" I asked in surprise. "She's in the red group. That's just one group ahead of Robbie and his bully friends. They can't count past ten because they run out of fingers."

"Before we get into how she knew about it, can you explain what it is we're talking about?" Stephanie asked.

Justin went on to explain factorials, which were

pretty easy to understand. A factorial is written with an exclamation point after the number and all it means is to multiply the number by all the numbers less than it. So, 4! = 4 × 3 × 2 × 1 = 24.

That looks like it could really be the answer! We knew it was when we figured out that 3! = 3 × 2 × 1, which is equal to 6. Boom, there was the answer for using three 1s to get to 6! We just had to get to 3 and use a factorial. And to get to 3, all we had to do was add the three 1s:

$$(1 + 1 + 1)! = 3! = 6$$

High fives all around. Catherine was right! Factorials were the answer.

"That's great for the ones, but how is that going to work for zeroes?" I asked. "Zero factorial is just going to be zero again, so we're still stuck."

Stephanie and I were discouraged, but Justin had a big smile on his face.

"Spill it," I said.

"Spill what?" he asked innocently.

"You know exactly what I'm talking about. You know something you're not telling us."

"Me? I don't know anything," Justin said, but I could tell he did.

"No cookies for you unless you tell us what you know."

With that threat, Justin had to give in. "What if zero factorial isn't equal to zero?" he asked slyly.

"How could it be anything but zero?" Stephanie

asked.

"My dad explained it to me," Justin said. "He said factorials are used to figure out how many ways you can arrange the things in a group. For example, there are three of us. How many ways can we stand in a line?"

I wrote the combinations down on a sheet of paper.

Jordan, Justin, Stephanie
Jordan, Stephanie, Justin
Justin, Jordan, Stephanie
Justin, Stephanie, Jordan
Stephanie, Justin, Jordan
Stephanie, Jordan, Justin

"There are six ways to do it," I said.

"That's right! Three people and six ways to arrange them, so three factorial equals six. Three times two times one," Justin said.

"That's really cool," Stephanie said.

"I agree," I said, "but it doesn't explain why zero factorial is one."

"How many ways can you arrange zero people in a line?" Justin asked.

"That doesn't make any sense," Stephanie said. "How can you arrange zero people?"

"I guess there's only one way," I said. "One empty line."

"Exactly!" Justin said. "So, zero factorial equals one."

"I don't know," Stephanie said. "Still seems kind of strange to me."

"Well, strange or not, it solves the last part of The Sixes Problem," Justin said.

"How?" I asked.

"Simple. If zero factorial is just one—" Justin started.

"Then we can use zero factorial three times to get one plus one plus one," Stephanie finished.

"And that leaves us with three, and we know that three factorial is—" Justin began.

"Six!" I shouted.

I wrote the equation on the board:

$$(0! + 0! + 0!)! = 3! = 6$$

"Ha! Take that, Mrs. Gouche. The Math Kids strike again!"

We had done it. We'd solved all the numbers in The Sixes Problem!

Justin didn't look pleased, though. Stephanie noticed and asked him why he wasn't happy to solve the problem.

"Oh, I'm happy we solved it," he said. "It's just that we didn't do it on our own. We needed help from someone else. And not just anyone, either. Someone from the red math group."

We thought about that for a moment. It didn't really matter to me that we had some outside help, but I guess I could see Justin's point. We had cracked the Prime-Time burglar case all by ourselves, but this time we had needed help from someone outside of our club.

"I've got a solution for that," Stephanie said.

Justin and I looked at her with raised eyebrows.

"Let's ask her to join the club," Stephanie said.

"Are you kidding me?" Justin asked. "She's in the red group!"

"Yeah, that's weird, isn't it?" Stephanie asked. "How can she be in the red group and still know cool stuff like factorials? It doesn't make any sense."

"Well, don't ask me. I don't know anything about her," I said.

"Then I'm going to make it my job to find out," Stephanie said.

CHAPTER 3

Monday rolled around again. Mrs. Gouche was surprised to see that we had finished The Sixes Problem.

"Nice job on this," she said. "You even got the tough ones; zero, one, and eight are usually the ones that stump people."

I was happy to accept her praise, but Justin was still a little grumpy about not solving the problem on our own.

As for Stephanie, she was on a mission to find out everything she could about Catherine Duchesne. Stephanie usually sat with us at lunchtime, but today I watched her go over to the table in the corner where Catherine sat all by herself. She was wearing a Josh Bell baseball jersey with a large 55 on the back. She was sketching a picture on a piece of notebook paper.

"Hey, nice picture," Stephanie said.

Catherine looked up in surprise and quickly slid the paper back into her notebook.

"Thanks," she responded softly.

"Can I sit with you?" Stephanie asked.

"I guess," Catherine answered.

Stephanie sat across from Catherine. Neither said anything for a minute. Stephanie opened her lunch box to see what her mom had packed. Catherine picked at her food, not looking up at Stephanie.

"Thanks for telling us about factorials," Stephanie said.

Catherine just nodded.

"We couldn't have done it without you," Stephanie continued.

Catherine nodded again.

"I'm Stephanie."

"I'm Catherine, with a C."

"Where did you learn about factorials?" Stephanie asked.

"I guess I read it in a math book."

"Well, I'm glad you did. We were really stuck."

"I saw it right away," Catherine said. "I wish we got problems like that in our math group."

"I was going to ask you about that," Stephanie said. "How come you're in the red group?"

Catherine shrugged her shoulders but didn't answer.

The rest of the lunch went pretty much the same way. Stephanie would ask a question and Catherine would say little or nothing. Sometimes she just nodded or shook her head. When the bell rang for the start of recess, Stephanie hadn't learned anything at all about the mysterious Catherine Duchesne.

As it turned out, we soon had other things on our

minds. During math group that afternoon, Mrs. Gouche dropped a bombshell on the three of us.

"The district is holding a Math Olympics competition this spring," she announced. "Teams from each of the fourth-grade rooms will be competing to see who represents McNair."

"When is the competition?" I asked excitedly.

"The fourth-grade rooms will compete in four weeks, so you'll want to get started practicing right away," she answered.

"What's the first step?" I asked. "What kind of problems will we be solving? How much time do we have? Will we—"

"Hold on a minute, Jordan," Mrs. Gouche said. "First, you need to find a fourth member for your team. Each team has to have two boys and two girls."

Justin and I looked dismayed. We already had a team. We didn't need anybody else.

Stephanie had another thought, and she blurted it out.

"Catherine Duchesne," she said.

Mrs. Gouche looked surprised. Justin and I did, too.

"I was thinking about Susie McDonald," said Mrs. Gouche.

No! Justin and I didn't say it out loud, but if we had, we would have shouted it.

"What about Catherine?" Stephanie asked.

"These are really tough problems," Mrs. Gouche said. "You know she's in the red math group, don't you?"

Of course we knew that. We had just had a big discussion about her on Saturday.

"Yes, but I've got a good feeling about her," Stephanie persisted.

"Well, we don't have to turn in the team's names until the end of the week, so think about it and let me know on Thursday. My recommendation is to go with Susie."

The competition, and the subject of the fourth person on the team, was all we talked about as we walked home that afternoon.

"We can't have Susie on the team," Justin said.

"You know my choice would be Catherine, but what do you have against Susie?" Stephanie asked.

Stephanie was kind of new to our school, so I explained it to her. Susie's mom is the president of the Parent Teacher Organization and I've heard my parents say that Mrs. McDonald thinks she rules the school. Because of her, Susie and her little brother Adam always get whatever they want. Susie got the lead solo in the school pageant when she was only in the third grade. Adam is the only second grader who starts every game on his soccer team, even though there are lots of kids who are better players. I wondered if Mrs. Gouche recommended Susie for our team because she is afraid of what Mrs. McDonald might do if she didn't.

"I'm not sure I could convince Catherine to join the team anyway," Stephanie said, "so it looks like we might be stuck with Susie."

Justin nodded sadly. "If Susie wants to be on the team, we're definitely stuck with her," he said. "Mrs. McDonald will see to that."

"Unless…" I said.

"Unless what?" Justin asked.

"Unless we can come up with a plan," I said.

"What did you have in mind?" Stephanie asked.

I didn't have a clue. I just knew we only had four days to convince Susie she didn't want to be on the team, and to convince Catherine that she did.

CHAPTER 4

On Tuesday morning, Mrs. Gouche had a couple surprises for us. First, she moved our math group from the afternoon to the morning. That was fine with me. I'd do math all day long if I could. It sure beat English and social studies—not exactly my best subjects. The second surprise, however, was not fine. Mrs. Gouche moved Susie into the yellow math group. I could tell from the look on Justin's face that he didn't like it one little bit. I didn't either.

"I thought if Susie was going to be on your math team, then we should move her into your group so she can practice with you," said Mrs. Gouche.

So that was the way she was going to play it! She wasn't really giving us a choice on who we wanted on our team. I bet that Mrs. McDonald had already talked to our teacher about it. Now we were really stuck!

I glanced over at Justin, saw him make a face, and knew he had been thinking the same thing.

"Here's a practice problem for you guys to work on

today," Mrs. Gouche said. "There are a thousand people at a concert. Can you prove that there are at least two people who have the same first and last initials?"

WAIT! DO YOU WANT TO TRY TO SOLVE THIS PUZZLE BEFORE SEEING IF THE MATH KIDS CAN DO IT? CAN YOU PROVE THAT AT LEAST TWO PEOPLE AT THE CONCERT HAVE THE SAME FIRST AND LAST INITIALS? GOOD LUCK!

"That's easy," said Susie.

We all looked at her in surprise. Maybe we had misjudged her math knowledge after all.

"Can you prove it?" Justin asked.

"Sure, it's easy. All you have to do is go to each person at the concert and get their initials," Susie answered, "and then compare all of them together to see if any of them match."

We just stared at her. Susie seemed quite proud of her solution. I didn't have the heart to tell her how ridiculous it really was. Stephanie didn't have a problem telling her how she felt, though.

"That's silly," she said.

Susie looked at her in surprise.

"How else are you going to know for sure if you don't ask them?"

"It's a math problem, so you have to use math," said Justin.

"Well, I'm sticking with my idea until you come up with something better," Susie said in a huff. She refused to work with us on coming up with a solution to the problem using math.

"Do you think factorials would work here?" I asked. "Isn't this kind of like finding out how many combinations there are?"

"Maybe," said Stephanie doubtfully, "but I think there's something more here."

Justin was looking at the problem. He had written it down as Mrs. Gouche described it. "She mentioned a thousand people," he said, "so that number must be important."

Justin is great at pulling out the important pieces of information from a problem. Lots of times there are other things in the problem that don't help you solve it, so you need to figure out which pieces are important and which ones aren't. Justin is a whiz at that!

He wrote 1,000 on the whiteboard. He also wrote 26.

"What's the 26 for?" Susie asked.

Justin gave her a long look before responding. "There are twenty-six letters in the alphabet."

"So?" she asked.

"So, there are twenty-six possible first initials and twenty-six possible last initials," he said.

"That would make twenty-six times twenty-six combinations of first and last initials," I said.

Stephanie did the math on the whiteboard. "That's six hundred seventy-six possible combinations for first and last initials."

"And since there are a thousand people, at least two of them must have the same initials," I said.

"But how do you know that without asking them?" Susie asked.

"Since one thousand is bigger than six hundred seventy-six, there must be at least two people who share the same initials," I explained.

"I don't get it," Susie said.

"Isn't it obvious?" Justin asked.

"Not to me, it isn't." Susie glared at Justin.

I tried to explain it to her. "There are six hundred seventy-six combinations of initials. A. A., A. B., A. C., and so on, then B. A., B. B., B. C., and so on, all the way up to Z. Z. Make sense so far?"

Susie nodded, but she didn't look very confident.

"So, let's say the first six hundred seventy-six people each have a unique combination of initials, from A. A. to Z. Z."

Justin and Stephanie were nodding along with my explanation, but Susie looked confused.

I don't think she was following my explanation, but I finished anyway. "When the next person comes up, they must have the same initials as someone else because we've already used up all of the possible combinations."

"So even if there were only six hundred seventy-seven people, at least two must have the same initials," Stephanie said.

"I still think it would be easier to ask everyone," Susie said with a pout.

"But that's not proving it!" Justin protested.

I could tell Susie and Justin were getting ready to argue, but Mrs. Gouche came over just in time to head it off.

"How's it coming?" she asked.

"We got it solved," said Stephanie, and went through the explanation for Mrs. Gouche.

"Very nice," Mrs. Gouche said. "That problem is an example of something called—"

The lunch bell rang, cutting her off. The students scrambled for the door, and Mrs. Gouche stopped in the middle of her sentence to restore order in the classroom.

At lunch, Stephanie sat down with Catherine Duchesne, who was once again sitting by herself at a table in the far corner of the cafeteria. This time she was wearing a Jarrett Jack basketball jersey. Like the baseball jersey she had been wearing the day before, this one also had a big 55 on the back. This time, Catherine was the first to speak up.

"You guys were doing a pigeonhole problem in math group, weren't you?" she said.

"What kind of problem did you call it?" Stephanie asked.

"Pigeonhole," Catherine responded. "It's a kind of problem where you can prove something by showing there are more pigeons than there are holes to put them in. If there are seven pigeons and only six pigeon holes, you can prove that at least one hole must have at least two pigeons in it. It's like the sock problem."

"What's the sock problem?"

"You're in a dark room. You open a drawer to get a pair of socks. You know there are ten red socks and ten blue socks. How many socks do you have to pull out before you know you have a pair?"

"Eleven," Stephanie blurted out.

Catherine smiled. "Lots of people would say that, but it's really only three. If you have three socks, you must have either three of one color, or two of one color and one of the other."

"I get it. Either way, you will have a pair," Stephanie said.

Catherine smiled and nodded. "Now, if you wanted to guarantee you have a pair of blue socks, you would need to pull out twelve socks, because the first ten might all be red."

Stephanie nodded thoughtfully. "Catherine, can I ask you a question?"

"I guess," Catherine said carefully.

"Why aren't you in the yellow math group?"

The smile faded from Catherine's face. She didn't say anything and instead went back to slowly eating her sandwich.

"Hey, I didn't mean to make you mad," Stephanie said. "It's just that you're so good at math, I'm a little surprised."

Catherine slowly took another bite. When she finished chewing, she finally answered but did it without looking up at Stephanie.

"Girls aren't good at math," she said quietly.

"What?" Stephanie said in surprise. "Who told you that?"

The recess bell rang. If Catherine answered, it was impossible to hear her quiet voice over the buzzing hive of activity, as students dropped their trash in the bins and headed toward the playground. Stephanie looked at the crowd pushing out the door, and, when she looked back, Catherine was gone.

CHAPTER 5

S tephanie didn't get another chance to talk to Catherine the rest of the day. Justin, Stephanie, and I walked home together.

"We're down to two days," Justin said with concern.

"We need to get rid of Susie and add Catherine," Stephanie said. "She said girls aren't good at math, but she's a whiz. She knew all about the problem we were solving this morning. She called it a pigeonhole problem."

"Why is it called a pigeonhole problem?" I asked.

"Later. What's important right now is getting her to join the team," said Stephanie.

"But if we can't talk her into joining, what can we do?" I asked.

"I still have two days to work on her," Stephanie said with determination. "I'm going to convince her to join us. Your job is to find a way to get Susie to drop out."

She cut through the yard across the street from my house and was gone. Justin and I sat on my front porch and tried to figure out a plan.

"If we can't get Catherine, maybe we can just have Susie keep quiet during the tournament," I said.

"When have you ever seen Susie with her mouth shut?" Justin asked.

I laughed, but Justin had a good point. Susie was always talking—before school, after school, and even during school. Anyone else would get in trouble for that, but Susie never did. I was sure Mrs. McDonald made sure of that. Since we couldn't get Susie replaced, we needed a way to get her to leave on her own.

And then a crazy idea popped into my head.

"Shirts!" I blurted out.

"Shirts?"

"We'll get team math shirts made for the tournament," I said.

"And how does that help us?" Justin asked.

"Because if there is one thing Susie likes better than talking, it's looking cool."

"So?"

"So, we'll make the most uncool shirts ever!"

For the next twenty minutes, we went through every bad math joke we had ever heard, trying to find the perfect saying to go on our team shirt:

THERE'S A FINE LINE BETWEEN NUMERATOR AND DENOMINATOR.

WHY WAS THE MATH BOOK SAD? IT HAD SO MANY PROBLEMS.

YOU MUST BE ODD TO BE NUMBER ONE!

MATH: THE ONLY SUBJECT THAT COUNTS.

MY TEACHER SAYS PI R SQUARED, BUT I KNOW PIE IS ROUND.

HOW DO YOU COUNT THE ANIMALS MOOING IN A FIELD? WITH A COW-CULATOR.

I HAVE A MATHEMATICAL CLOCK—IT ARITHMA-TICKS.

WHAT STATE CALCULATES THE BEST? MATH-ACHUSSETS.

Yes, the jokes were bad, but that was the point. We wanted to come up with something that Susie would absolutely hate. It was the perfect plan!

Except that it wasn't. The next day, when we told Susie we were planning on math shirts for the tournament, she loved the idea. She even loved the bad math puns, although I think there were some she didn't even understand. We were back to the drawing board, and now we were down to just one day.

In the meantime, Stephanie was still working on Catherine. For the third day in a row, Stephanie joined Catherine in the far corner of the cafeteria for lunch. This time she was wearing a football jersey for Brandon Graham. Again, there was a big 55 on the back.

"You know that girls are just as good as boys in math, don't you?" Stephanie asked.

Catherine nodded.

"I mean, you know more math than any boy in the class"—Stephanie paused to see who was around—"and that includes Justin and Jordan."

Catherine smiled and gave a little shrug of her shoulders.

"So how come you said girls aren't good at math?" Stephanie asked.

"That's what my dad always says," Catherine answered quietly.

"Well, your dad is wrong!" Stephanie said. "You're really good at math, and I think you know it."

Catherine nodded again.

Stephanie could see that Catherine wanted to say more, so she waited.

After a long silence, Catherine finally spoke again. "My dad teaches math at the college. He always tells me that the boys in his math classes are much better than the girls."

"Do you believe him?" Stephanie asked.

"I guess it must be true because he says it all the time."

"Well, it isn't. There are lots of women mathematicians. Have you ever heard of Grace Hopper?"

Catherine shook her head no.

"She was one of the first computer programmers. She was also an admiral in the navy and even got a ship named after her."

"Really?" Catherine asked.

"Really," Stephanie answered. "And then there's Joan Clarke, who was on the team that broke the German Enigma Code machine in the Second World War and saved millions of lives. And Maryam Mirzakhani was the first woman to win the Fields Medal, which is the highest honor for a mathematician."

"Wow, how do you know so much about this?" Catherine asked in amazement.

"My dad tells me about them all the time," Stephanie answered. "He thinks it's really cool that I like math."

"I wish my dad felt the same way."

"How about your mom? What does she say?"

Catherine just looked down at the table. "My mom died when I was little."

"Oh, I'm so sorry, Catherine."

Neither girl said anything for a few minutes—just slowly ate their lunch.

"Well, your dad is wrong," Stephanie said, breaking the silence. "And we've got to find a way to make him believe that."

"But how?" Catherine asked.

"By joining our team and winning that math tournament."

"But I thought Susie was on your team."

"Not for long," Stephanie said. "What do you say? If we get her to drop out, will you do it?"

The smile on Catherine's face said it all.

But that still didn't solve our problem.

"It doesn't matter if Catherine is in," I said glumly as we walked home from school. "We also need Susie to be out."

Justin and Stephanie didn't have anything to say the rest of the way home. We were down to one day, and no one had any ideas on how to get Susie off the team.

CHAPTER 6

"There must be a way to get Susie out of the picture," Justin said as we walked to school the next day.

"Do you think we should ask her to leave the team?" Stephanie asked.

"Nah, she'd never do it," Justin replied.

"It doesn't matter," I said, feeling defeated. "We've run out of time. We have to let Mrs. Gouche know today."

"Well, I say we tell her we chose Catherine!" Stephanie said defiantly.

"You don't know Susie's mom," Justin said. "If Susie wants to be on the team, Mrs. McDonald will make sure it happens. We need Susie to drop out herself."

"But how?" Stephanie asked.

"I think I have an idea," I said. "It's a little crazy though."

"I wouldn't have expected anything else," Justin said with a grin.

As I started to explain, the first warning bell sounded. Class started in five minutes. We had run out of time.

But it turned out we were in luck.

When we walked into the classroom, someone else was sitting at Mrs. Gouche's desk. We had a substitute! Normally, that meant the bullies ran the class for the day, and that day was no different. Our sub was a sweet little old lady named Mrs. Anderson. She tried to take control, but I could tell it wasn't going to happen.

"Okay, class, let's settle down so I can take attendance," she said. "When I call your name, please raise your hand. Bryce Bookerman?"

Bryce looked at the sub but did not raise his hand. There were a couple giggles.

"Bill Cape?"

Bill's hand remained on his desk. A few more kids were laughing now.

"Quiet down, please," she said, looking sternly at the class. "Robert Colson?"

Robbie smiled but didn't raise his hand. Now most of the class was laughing. I could tell the sub was getting frustrated.

"If you are here, I need you to raise your hand or I'll have to mark you down as absent. Robert Colson?"

Robbie continued to smile but still didn't raise his hand.

Mrs. Anderson looked directly at Robbie. "Is your name Robert Colson?" she asked.

Robbie smiled at her and said, "No, ma'am. My name is Robbie Colson."

The entire class broke into laughter.

It took almost thirty minutes for Mrs. Anderson to finish taking attendance. By then, she was so flustered, we knew there would be no learning that day. She handed out some social studies worksheets and told us to work quietly at our desks.

"Can we work in small groups if we're quiet?" I asked.

She gave me a long look before finally nodding.

Stephanie, Justin, and I took three empty desks near the back of the room.

"Okay, what's your idea?" Stephanie asked as soon as we were alone.

I quietly told them my plan. Midway through, Stephanie started to smile. When I was done, we were all grinning from ear to ear.

"You were right," Justin said. "It's a little crazy, but since it's all we've got let's give it a shot."

"It's going to take some teamwork—and a little cooperation from Mrs. Anderson," I said.

We looked up at our substitute teacher, who looked like she had her hands full with the bullies, who were in the middle of a game of trash can basketball.

"Oh, I think she'll cooperate," Stephanie said.

We huddled together for another twenty minutes, working out the details of the plan. Then Stephanie raised her hand and asked if she could be excused to use the restroom.

"Are students allowed to be in the hallway by themselves?" Mrs. Anderson asked.

"Yes, ma'am. You just need to sign a permission slip," Stephanie said politely. She handed Mrs. Anderson a blank slip.

"What information do I need to include?" the sub asked.

"I can fill it out if that would be easier for you," Stephanie said. "I just need your signature at the bottom."

Mrs. Anderson looked at Stephanie, who gazed back at the teacher with an innocent smile on her face. When Mrs. Anderson turned her back, Stephanie wrote *Computer Lab* in the space marked *Destination*. She gave a small nod to Justin and me and quietly left the classroom.

When Stephanie returned, she slipped a USB thumb drive into my hand, and now it was my turn. I asked Mrs. Anderson if I could take the attendance sheet to the principal's office. Mrs. Anderson looked grateful.

"I'll need a permission slip, too," I said. "If you just sign it, I can fill out the rest of it."

Mrs. Anderson thanked me and signed the form. I nodded to Stephanie and Justin and slipped into the hallway. I ducked into the restroom and completed the form, filling in *Copy Room* for the destination.

I almost got cold feet when I saw the principal, but she just waved her hand in my direction and continued down the hallway. I was glad to see that the copy room was empty, but I knew I needed to work fast. I had made copies for Mrs. Gouche before, so I entered her code into the photocopier. I pulled the thumb drive Stephanie had given me from my pocket and pushed it firmly into the USB port on the copier. I selected the file to print and chose one hundred for the number of copies. I was about to push the *Print* button when Coach Harder, the gym teacher, walked into the room.

He looked at me suspiciously.

"Are you supposed to be in here?" he asked.

"Um, yes sir. Mrs. Gouche needs some worksheets printed," I stammered.

"Mrs. Gouche? I thought she was out sick today," he said, staring directly into my eyes.

"Um, I mean for her sub."

"I see. How many copies are you printing?"

I couldn't make anything up because Coach Harder could easily look down and see the number I had selected.

"A hundred," I answered.

"A hundred, huh? Well, would you mind if I jumped in front of you? I just need two copies of this form."

"No sir. Go for it."

I pressed the *Clear* button before Coach Harder had a chance to look at the name of the file I was printing. He made his copies and was out the door without another word. I quickly reentered the information and clicked *Print*. The machine hummed into action and I watched the sheets start to fill up the tray. I pulled one of them out and read it while the machine continued to work. I smiled at the great job Stephanie had done.

Luckily, no one else came in before the last copy landed with a whisper in the tray. I picked up the copies and headed back toward my classroom.

Now came the tricky part. I had left the room to take the attendance form to the office. I had no way to explain why I was coming back with a hundred neatly printed sheets of paper. This is where I needed Justin— and a little help from the bullies.

Mrs. Anderson looked over as I opened the classroom door. The stack of papers was still hidden by the door, but I only had a few seconds before she would notice. That's when Justin launched his attack, using a rubber band to fire a pencil eraser at Robbie's head. It was a direct hit! Robbie yelled, drawing Mrs. Anderson's attention. He was already out of his chair and headed for Justin as I slipped into the room. The room exploded into chaos as Robbie tried to catch Justin. All the bullies were in motion now, trying to corner Justin, who dodged behind desks to keep away from them. Justin was the smallest kid in the class, but his small size allowed him to slip through places the bigger kids couldn't. Stephanie managed to trip Bill Cape as he rounded a corner, and he went down with a crash. Mrs. Anderson was yelling for everyone to get back to their seats. With all the noise and activity, no one noticed as I quietly placed the stack of papers into my backpack.

Part one of the plan was complete, but would it work?

CHAPTER 7

On Friday morning, Justin, Stephanie, and I left early for school and arrived just after Old Mike, the school janitor, opened the front door of the school. He greeted us with his normal big smile.

"You kids are here early today. Just can't get enough of school, huh?"

"You sure know us, Old Mike," I replied.

"What's that you got there?" he asked, pointing to the stack of papers I had printed the day before.

"Oh, just some flyers we're going to put up around the school," Stephanie said.

We moved on before the friendly janitor could ask any more questions. We split up. Stephanie and Justin took both sides of the main hallway, while I tackled the announcement boards at the front of the school. In twenty minutes, we had taped the flyers all up and down the hallway. We saved a handful for our own classroom: two on the whiteboard at the front of the room, two on the door, and one on Susie's chair.

When we had finished putting up the flyers, we retreated to the school cafeteria to wait. We didn't want anyone to suspect we had anything to do with the flyers. It also gave us a good way to avoid Robbie and his buddies, who were still angry from the day before. It looked like our truce with the bullies was over.

When our math group met, Susie took her place next to Stephanie. Justin and I looked at each other. It didn't seem like the plan had worked.

"Okay, first things first," said Mrs. Gouche. "We need to get your team submitted for the competition."

She started to write our names on the competition entry form, but Susie interrupted her.

"Mrs. Gouche?" she said hesitantly.

"Yes, Susie?"

"I can't be in the competition," she said.

"But why?" Mrs. Gouche asked in surprise.

Susie held up one of the flyers we had created. The teacher read it and looked up at Susie.

"A singing contest?" she asked.

"Yes, and it's on the same day as the math competition," Susie explained.

Justin, Stephanie, and I all put our hands over our mouths to hide our smiles. My crazy plan had actually worked!

"But who can we get to take your place, Susie?" Stephanie asked innocently.

"What about Catherine?" Susie asked.

I almost laughed out loud. Not only had the plan worked, but Susie had even suggested Catherine as her replacement!

"I guess she'd be okay," I said, barely managing to stifle my giggles. "Could she be moved to our math group, so we can practice together?"

Mrs. Gouche nodded, and, just like that, Susie went back to the blue math group, Catherine moved from the red to the yellow group, and we had our team. We huddled together in the back corner and giggled about our plan for getting Susie to drop off the team.

"How did you know she would fall for it?" Catherine asked.

"Hey, it's a math contest," I said. "I took a calculated risk."

Everyone groaned, but their smiles told me my joke wasn't half bad.

Now it was time to get to work. We had three weeks to go. Would we be ready?

Unfortunately, we had another problem we had to solve first. The bullies were still mad at Justin for shooting the pencil eraser at Robbie's head. Robbie and Bill had both received three days of detention for chasing Justin around the room. Now they were looking for revenge!

"I'll be waiting for you in the parking lot," Robbie whispered angrily as he passed Justin's desk.

Justin looked worried, and I could understand why.

Robbie was the biggest boy in the class and towered over Justin. And if that wasn't enough of a problem, Robbie never faced off against someone by himself. His gang of bullies was always by his side. On the other side of the room, Bill Cape raised a fist in my direction. Two seats in front of me, Bryce turned and gave me a sneer.

I looked at the clock and saw that the three o'clock dismissal bell would ring in just a couple of minutes. Whatever idea we were going to come up with, we'd better do it quickly.

I raised my hand. When Mrs. Gouche called on me, I put on my sweet and innocent face and asked her if I could help take her things to her car after school was over.

"Why, thank you, Jordan," she said. "I do have a lot of things to carry today, so that would be a big help."

"My friends and I can help, too," Robbie said, giving me an evil smile.

"Wow, everyone is being so helpful today," Mrs. Gouche said. "Okay, Jordan, if you, Robbie, Bryce, and Bill can meet me at the front of the room after the bell rings, that would be great."

Great. All I did was delay my fate for a couple extra minutes. As soon as we loaded her car, Mrs. Gouche would drive away, and I'd be stuck in the parking lot with the bullies.

That's when Justin came to my rescue.

"But Jordan, didn't you promise Old Mike that we'd help him take down all of the old flyers from the bulletin boards?" he asked.

"Oh, that's right," I replied, although I had no idea what Justin was talking about.

"That's okay," said Mrs. Gouche. "You and Justin can help Mr. Watson with the bulletin boards. I'll have enough help with Robbie, Bryce, and Bill."

The looks from the bullies were fierce. We'd beaten them once again. They were stuck helping Mrs. Gouche out to her car while Justin and I were free to escape out the school's side door and be out of sight before they knew we were gone.

And we had almost made it out when we ran into Joe Christian.

Joe is one of the smartest kids in the fourth grade— maybe in the whole school. He skipped third grade and is still smarter than most of the kids in Miss Herschel's fourth-grade class. He is good in every subject, but math is his best by far. There is no doubt he is smart. The problem is he loves to tell everyone how smart he is.

"I heard you two are on the math team for your class," he said.

"Yeah, along with Stephanie and Catherine," I answered.

"Do you really think you have a chance against my team?"

"Who else is on your team?"

"Does it really matter?" he asked with a laugh. "I could beat your whole team by myself."

Like I said, Joe loves to brag about how smart he is.

"Well, I guess we'll just have to wait and see," I said without much confidence in my voice.

Joe laughed and walked away.

Justin and I walked home slowly. We were smart enough to outwit the bullies, but could we beat Joe in a math competition? I had my doubts.

CHAPTER 8

While Justin and I were making our escape from the bullies, Catherine and Stephanie were walking home together.

"What got you interested in math?" Stephanie asked. "Your dad?"

"Well, he definitely talks about math a lot—like, all the time," Catherine said, "but it was art that really got me into math."

"Art? What does art have to do with math?"

"Everything," Catherine answered. "C'mon, follow me."

Catherine led Stephanie down a side street to a small park. Some younger kids were playing on the playground and their laughter echoed off the trees. Catherine gestured toward a bed of flowers lining the path.

"What am I looking for?" Stephanie asked.

"The math," Catherine said cryptically.

Stephanie looked at the flowers in the bed. They

were beautiful, a mixture of a bunch of different types of flowers and colors, but she didn't see anything that looked at all like math.

"These are lilies," Catherine said, pointing to a small patch of delicate white flowers. "Count the petals."

"Three," Stephanie said.

"And these are buttercups." Catherine pointed to a clump of beautiful yellow flowers.

"Five petals," said Stephanie.

Another point, this time to a bunch of bright orange flowers. Stephanie had to bend over to count the petals, breathing in the wonderful scent as she did.

"Thirteen, I think."

"That's right. Marigolds have thirteen petals. Okay, last one," Catherine said, pointing to a white flower with a beautiful orange center. "The daisy."

Stephanie counted the petals on one, then a second. Both came out to the same number.

"Thirty-four!" she said.

"That's right." Catherine smiled. "See, there's math all around us."

"Wait, I don't get it," Stephanie said in confusion. "The flowers are beautiful, but where's the math?"

Catherine sat on a bench and opened her backpack. She removed a notebook and a sharpened pencil.

"Have you ever heard of the Fibonacci sequence?" she asked as Stephanie joined her on the bench.

"No."

"Then you're in for a treat!" Catherine said with excitement. "The first two numbers in the sequence are one and one. You get the next number in the sequence by adding the last two numbers. To get the third number, you add one and one to get two. To get the fourth number, you add one and two to get three. The sequence keeps going like that. Here's what the first few numbers of the sequence look like."

Catherine wrote the numbers in her notebook:

1, 1, 2, 3, 5, 8, 13, 21, 34,...

"Recognize any of these numbers?" she asked.

At first, Stephanie didn't get it, then a gleam came to her eye as she saw what Catherine what trying to show her.

"The petals! The numbers of petals on the flowers are all Fibonacci numbers!"

Catherine smiled and nodded. She reached into her backpack and pulled out a sheet of graph paper.

"And that's not all. If I make squares for each of the numbers—one by one, two by two, three by three, and so on—I'll end up with something like this," she said.

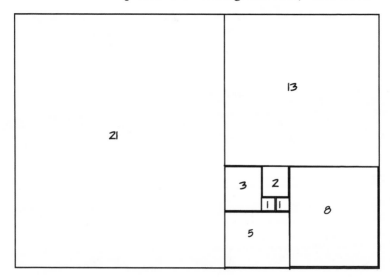

"That's really cool that all of the squares fit together like that," Stephanie said.

"Oh, that's not all they do," Catherine said as she pulled a red marker out of her backpack. "Look what happens when I connect the squares together."

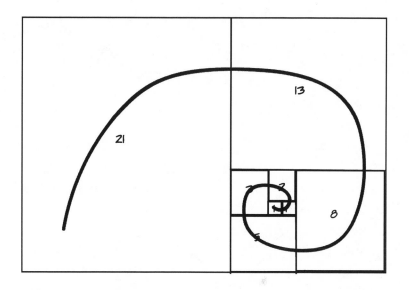

"Do you recognize that shape?" Catherine asked.

"It looks familiar, but—"

"Think about the shape of a ram's horn, or a seashell, or a hurricane."

Stephanie's eyes grew wide. "You're right!" she exclaimed. "It does look like a seashell. But I'm still not sure where the art part fits in."

"I was just getting to that," Catherine said as she pulled another piece of paper out of her backpack. "Here's the Fibonacci sequence again."

She wrote the numbers across the top of the paper:

1, 1, 2, 3, 5, 8, 13, 21, 34,...

"Now look what happens when we start dividing the numbers in the sequence." She did the calculations using her phone:

$$1 \div 1 = 1$$
$$2 \div 1 = 2$$
$$3 \div 2 = 1.5$$
$$5 \div 3 = 1.667$$
$$8 \div 5 = 1.6$$
$$13 \div 8 = 1.625$$
$$21 \div 13 = 1.615$$
$$34 \div 21 = 1.619$$

"As you keep going, the numbers get closer and closer to 1.618," Catherine said.

"So, what's that have to do with art?" Stephanie asked.

"That number is called the golden ratio," Catherine explained. "It's used in geometry, architecture, and yes, even art. For example, if you look at the famous picture of the *Mona Lisa*, you'll find that the length of her head is 1.618 times the width of her head. You'll also find the golden ratio in many famous buildings, like the Parthenon in Greece."

"That's so cool," said Stephanie.

"You want to hear something really cool? There are always more female bees than male bees in a hive. When you divide the number of females by the number of male bees, guess what number you get."

"The golden ratio?" Stephanie guessed.

Catherine's broad smile was enough to tell Stephanie she had guessed right.

"C'mon, we'd better get going," Catherine said. "My dad will be wondering where I am."

Stephanie walked with Catherine all the way to her house, even though it was a little bit out of her way. Jordan and Justin were nice enough, she thought, but she was glad Catherine was now a member of the Math Kids.

As Stephanie turned to walk home, Catherine came running back out of her house.

"Hey, wait up!" she called to Stephanie.

Stephanie stopped and saw that Catherine had a tattered book in her hand.

"I thought you might enjoy this book," she said. "It's where I learned all about the Fibonacci sequence."

She handed the book to Stephanie with a shy smile, then turned and ran back up the porch steps to her house.

CHAPTER 9

On Monday, we discovered that Catherine was going to be a big boost to our math team. She certainly knew a lot of math, including some things the rest of us didn't know. For example, on one of the problems we were working on, we needed to multiply 65 times 65. Justin went to the whiteboard to do the math, but Catherine just blurted out the answer.

"It's 4,225," she said.

Justin turned from the board and stared at her. In fact, we all turned and looked at her.

"How did you get that so fast?" Justin asked.

"It's just a mental math trick my dad taught me when I was little," she said.

Of course, we wanted to know the trick, so she explained it to us.

"It's really easy," she said, "but it only works under certain conditions. First, it must be a two-digit number, and the tens digit must be the same for both numbers. Second, the two ones digits must add up to ten."

I checked out the conditions for 65 × 65. Both were two-digit numbers. The tens digit was 6 for both. The ones digits added up to 10. The conditions checked out.

"To get the last two numbers of the answer, just multiply the two ones digits together," Catherine explained. "We multiply five times five and we get twenty-five."

She wrote 25 on the whiteboard.

"Now, to get the first two numbers, multiply the tens digit by one more than the tens digit, so in this case we multiply six times seven to get forty-two," she said.

She wrote 42 in front of 25 and added a comma after the 4 to get 4,225. Just to prove it to himself, Justin multiplied it out by hand. Catherine was right!

We each had to try it out, of course. I multiplied 34 × 36 and quickly got 1,224. Stephanie went with 42 × 48 and got 2,016 in an instant. Justin, of course, had to push the trick to its limits, so he tried 93 × 97. He smiled broadly when his answer of 9,021 checked out.

"That's really cool, Catherine," Justin said.

Math group every day consisted of working problem after problem, trying to learn different techniques that would help us as the competition grew closer. We found that sometimes the best way to solve a problem was with some educated guessing. For example, one problem asked us to find three consecutive numbers that you can multiply together to get 15,600.

WAIT! DO YOU WANT TO TRY TO SOLVE THIS PUZZLE BEFORE SEEING IF THE MATH KIDS CAN DO IT? CAN YOU FIND THREE CONSECUTIVE NUMBERS WHOSE PRODUCT IS 15,600? GOOD LUCK!

At first, we didn't know how to even start with a problem like this. As it turned out, we were trying too hard to come up with a complicated approach when all we really needed to do was start guessing numbers.

"What if we just tried some numbers to see if we can narrow it down?" Stephanie suggested.

"That could take forever," Justin protested.

But it actually didn't take long at all. We started with multiplying 20 × 20 × 20 and got 8,000. That told us that 20 was too small. When we tried 30 × 30 × 30, we got 27,000, so we knew 30 was too large. We tried 25 × 25 × 25 and got 15,625. We were close. Since we needed three consecutive numbers, we tried 24 × 25 × 26 and got the answer we wanted! This was one of those cases where it was easier, and much quicker, to try out some possible solutions and see what we got.

This method, of course, didn't sit too well with Justin, who liked to be very logical when it came to solving math problems. To him, the thought of guessing answers seemed wrong. We tried to convince him that we really had taken a logical approach. We found an answer that was too small, then one that was too large, and then narrowed it down until we found the right one.

He was much happier about how we solved the next problem. We had to find five consecutive even numbers that added up to 320.

WAIT! DO YOU WANT TO TRY TO SOLVE THIS PUZZLE BEFORE SEEING IF THE MATH KIDS CAN DO IT? CAN YOU FIND FIVE CONSECUTIVE EVEN NUMBERS THAT ADD UP TO 320? GOOD LUCK!

Justin started by dividing 320 by 5 (since there were five numbers to add) and got an answer of 64. We decided that 64 must be the middle number, so we found two even numbers on both sides of 64 and added them. Our decision was correct:

$60 + 62 + 64 + 66 + 68 = 320$

Just like that, we had the answer.

"Now that's the way to solve a math problem!" Justin declared. "No guessing needed on that one."

We all agreed, but we also decided that sometimes guessing wasn't such a bad way to solve some problems.

While things were going really well with our preparations for the math competition, the rest of fourth grade went on pretty much as usual—unfortunately.

The bullies were back in action, doing their favorite tricks, like knocking things on the floor when they passed our desks, and tripping us when we passed by theirs. More than once I saw a spitball whiz by my head when Mrs. Gouche wasn't looking.

"Why do those guys always pick on you?" Catherine asked as we ate lunch in a corner of the cafeteria.

"It's not their fault," Justin said.

I looked at him in amazement. "How is it not their fault?"

"You'd be mean, too, if you had to look at their ugly faces in a mirror every morning," he replied with a grin.

We all laughed. A little too loudly, unfortunately, because it caught the attention of Robbie and Bill two tables over. Robbie looked around to make sure there weren't any teachers nearby and then stomped his way to our table, with Bill following closely behind him.

"Now, isn't this cute," he said. "There must be a loser convention in town."

Bill laughed like it was the funniest thing he had ever heard.

"I could find a better insult than that in a bowl of alphabet soup," Catherine said quietly as she stared straight at Robbie.

"What did you say?" Robbie yelled as he began to turn red with anger.

"Let me explain," Catherine said. "I'll try to say it sloooowly so you can understand."

"You better shut up, or, or, or—" Robbie stammered in anger.

"Or what, Robbie?" asked Coach Harder, who had come up quietly behind him.

"She was picking on Robbie," Bill said.

"Is that true, Robbie?" Coach Harder asked. "Is she picking on you?"

Catherine smiled sweetly at Robbie, making him even madder. But with Coach Harder standing right there, he was helpless to do anything.

"I didn't hear you, Robbie," Coach Harder said. "Was she picking on you?"

"No," Robbie said meekly.

"Then I suggest you and Bill get out to the playground," he said.

Robbie gave a furious look in our direction, then turned and walked away. When he was gone, Stephanie gave Catherine a high five.

"Nicely done, Catherine," she said.

It was amazing what a little confidence had done to Catherine. In just a few short days, she had gone from not saying a word to standing up to the bullies. Unfortunately, that meant Catherine was now on the bullies' bad side, and I knew from experience that their bad side was not a good place to be.

CHAPTER 10

The math competition was only five days away, and I was starting to feel like we had a pretty good chance to beat Joe Christian and his team. Joe was smart, but we were really starting to click as a team. We were working well together, with everyone helping to solve problems. Justin might get us started with a good idea, then Stephanie or I might come up with the next step, and then Catherine might finish the solution. The next problem, we would all contribute in a different way. Best of all, we were having a lot of fun!

And then it happened.

Tuesday morning, Catherine wasn't at school. We still managed to solve problems during our math group, but it was much tougher without her. On Wednesday morning, she was gone again. When Thursday morning came, and she still wasn't back at school, we started to worry. We couldn't seem to focus on any of the problems.

"Where could she be?" Stephanie asked.

"Probably sick," I guessed.

"She seemed fine on Monday afternoon after school," Stephanie said.

"Maybe she has food poisoning," Justin said.

"Or was hit by a car," I added.

Stephanie looked horrified. "Don't even think that!" she said angrily.

"What are we going to do if she's still missing on Saturday morning?" I asked. "Will they let us compete with just three people?"

"Well, I'm going to go by her house after school and see what's going on," Stephanie said.

Justin and I agreed to go with her, and we all met at the side door when school let out. We had only made it twenty feet from the door when I heard a screech of bike tires on the blacktop. I turned, and there they were—Robbie, Bill, Bryce, and Sniffy—the whole gang of bullies.

"Nowhere to go, is there?" Robbie taunted.

It was one of the few times Robbie was right. There wasn't anywhere we could run. They were between us and the school, and there was no way we could outrun them on their bikes.

"Where's your little friend?" Bill asked.

"Who are you talking about?" I asked innocently.

"You know exactly who he's talking about!" Robbie shouted. "She thinks she's pretty smart, doesn't she?"

"Actually, she is pretty smart," Stephanie said. "A lot smarter than you, that's for sure."

"That's not saying much," Justin said quietly.

"What did you say?" Robbie asked, filled with anger.

"I said it's not saying much to say Catherine is smarter than you," Justin said defiantly.

I was always amazed to see how brave Justin was. He sure wasn't letting his size stop him from standing up to one of the biggest kids in the entire school.

I could see that the bullies had had enough. They were closing in on us, and we were running out of time. I had an idea. I didn't for a second think it would work, but it was at least worth a shot.

Robbie was raising his fist in front of Justin, but he paused when I spoke.

"Don't you want to know where Catherine is?" I asked.

"Who cares?" Robbie answered.

"She's really sick," I said dramatically. "She might even die."

Now I had the attention of all the bullies.

"She might die?" asked Bryce.

"We all might," I answered.

"What do you mean?" asked Robbie.

"She has a rare tropical disease," I said.

"Yeah? How'd she get it?" asked Robbie.

"Her uncle brought her a parrot from South America," Stephanie said quickly. "He didn't know that parrots carry lots of diseases."

I could tell that a few of the bullies were starting to buy the story, but Robbie was still a little skeptical.

"So why would her disease affect you?" he asked.

"Once someone has the disease, anyone around them can catch it," Justin said. "We've probably got it since we hang around her."

"And the more time you spend around us, the more likely you'll get it, too," I added.

I walked toward the bullies. Sniffy, Bryce, and Bill rolled their bikes back two or three feet. Robbie stood his ground, but then he backed up, too, as Justin stepped toward him.

"Ah, you punks aren't worth the time," Robbie said with a sneer. "Come on, guys."

Robbie turned his bike and pedaled away quickly, followed closely by his little gang. Justin waited until they had gone around the corner of the school and were safely out of sight before he raised his hand to me for a high five.

"Nicely done, Jordan."

"A deadly parrot disease—that was your plan?" Stephanie asked.

"I just said deadly disease. You were the one who came up with the parrot," I said. "And it probably wouldn't have worked with anyone else, but those guys aren't the brightest light bulbs in the box."

"Okay, let's get over to Catherine's house and see what's really going on," Stephanie said.

When we got to Catherine's house, we were met at the door by a man wearing a suit. He looked at us suspiciously and asked what we wanted.

"Is Catherine home?" Stephanie asked. "We're friends of hers from school."

"She's not available," the man responded.

"Are you her—" Stephanie began, but the man closed the door in our faces.

"What was that all about?" I asked.

"That's what I'm going to find out," said Stephanie as she knocked loudly on the front door.

The man in the suit cracked the door open and saw it was us again.

"What do you want?" he asked.

"We're friends of Catherine's from school," Stephanie replied.

"You already told me that. And I said she's not available."

"Is she sick?" Stephanie asked.

"Did I say she was sick?" the man replied with a scowl on his face.

"No."

"That's right. I said she was unavailable. You know what that word means, right?"

"Yeah, I know what it means."

"Then let me repeat it. She is unavailable," the man said as he once again closed the door in our faces.

We stepped off the porch and retreated to the sidewalk.

"What do we do now?" Justin asked.

"I'll tell you what we're going to do," said Stephanie defiantly. "We're going to find Catherine.

She marched down the sidewalk away from Catherine's house.

"Where are you going?" I asked.

Stephanie didn't respond as she walked quickly down the sidewalk. Justin and I had to run to catch her at the corner.

"I've got to get home but meet me back here as soon as you're done with dinner," Stephanie said tersely.

"What's your plan?" Justin asked.

"Just trust me," she answered as she turned and started to jog toward her house.

After dinner, Justin and I walked back to the same corner. Stephanie was already there, impatiently pacing back and forth.

"It's about time," she said. "Let's go."

Without another word, Stephanie walked away quickly, with Justin and me following in her wake. She made a left-hand turn at the next corner and I thought I knew where she was going.

"You're going around the back of her house, aren't you?" I asked.

Stephanie didn't respond, but I knew I had guessed right when she walked between two houses midway down the block. She stopped at a row of bushes near the rear of Catherine's backyard. We all ducked behind the shrubbery so we couldn't be seen from the windows at the back of the house.

"What now?" Justin asked.

"Now we wait," Stephanie answered.

"Wait for what?" I asked.

"I don't know, but we need to do something," she said in frustration.

As it turned out, we didn't have to wait very long. We were watching the back of the house when we saw Catherine walk past the sliding glass door leading to the deck behind the house. She disappeared, but then we saw her again in another window. She stopped in front of the window and looked out into the backyard. Stephanie stood up and began to wave.

"What are you doing?" I said as I tried to pull her back down behind the bushes. "She'll see you!"

"That's the idea," Stephanie said.

Catherine finally noticed Stephanie waving her hands. Catherine took a quick glance around her, then quickly raised and lowered her hand several times.

"What does that mean?" Justin asked.

"She wants us to stay out of sight," Stephanie said excitedly.

We ducked behind the bushes. Twenty minutes later we heard the back door slide open. Peeking through the bushes, we saw Catherine throw something onto the deck. Whatever it was, it slid off the deck and into a flower bed. We heard a man's voice yelling and the sliding door slammed shut. The curtains swished closed, and we lost sight of Catherine.

We crouched behind the bushes until the sun had set and deep shadows fell over Catherine's backyard.

"It's time," Stephanie finally announced.

"Time for what?" I asked.

"Time to get whatever it is Catherine threw out the door."

Before we could stop her, Stephanie was running across the backyard. She was almost to the deck when a spotlight above the back door clicked on, shining brightly across the yard. Stephanie dove to the ground, half in and half out of the flower bed. The curtain parted, and we could see the man in the suit staring out. The back door opened, and he stepped out onto the deck. Stephanie lay frozen on the ground. She was out of sight but would be seen if the man took a couple more steps across the deck.

That's when Catherine came to the rescue.

"Hey!" she shouted from the back door.

The man in the suit turned. Catherine raised her hand and the backyard was plunged into darkness. Stephanie took that opportunity to make a run for it. She flew across the width of the deck, crouching low to remain as invisible as possible. The man in the suit reached into the doorway and flipped a switch. The backyard was once again filled with light. By that time, however, Stephanie had made it around the corner of the house and was safely hidden from view.

Justin and I sprinted back to the street and caught up with Stephanie at the end of Catherine's block. She was reading a crumpled sheet of paper in the glow of the streetlight.

"I'm calling an emergency meeting of the Math Kids!" she yelled as we approached. "Catherine's dad is in trouble, and we might be the only ones who can save him."

CHAPTER 11

The Math Kids met in Justin's basement.
Stephanie had the crumpled piece of paper she
had retrieved from Catherine's flower bed.

"Okay, what do you mean Catherine's dad is in
trouble?" I asked. "What does the note say?"

Stephanie laid the piece of paper on the table. Justin
peered over my shoulder as I read the note aloud.

Stephanie,

I hope you get this message. The guy in the suit is
from the FBI. My dad has been kidnapped. He's been
working on a math formula for the military, to help
them encrypt satellite messages. The FBI won't let me
out of the house. They said it's for my protection.

The kidnappers sent a ransom note. They want the
formula. My dad added a note at the bottom of the
ransom letter so the FBI would know he's still alive. I
think he added a code for me to find him. I can't solve
it by myself, so I hope you guys can help. Here's what
my dad wrote:

Stephanie,

I hope you get this message. The guy in the suit is from the FBI. My dad has been kidnapped. He's been working on a math formula for the military to help them encrypt satellite messages. The FBI won't let me out of the house. They said it's for my protection.

The kidnappers sent a ransom note. They want the formula. My dad added a note at the bottom of the ransom letter so the FBI would know he's still alive. I think he added a code for me to find him. I can't solve it by myself, so I hope you guys can help. Here's what my dad wrote:

Dear Catherine,

I won't tell you a _fib_: This has been an unfortunate _sequence_ of events, but I think you'll find where I am coming from when I say things will turn out fine. I am usually at a loss for words when it comes to situations like this, but in this case, one should cooperate fully and do what they say. I am in the middle of this problem but I'm sure I can find the right solution if I think hard enough. I hate being apart from you and I will fully cooperate with the kidnappers so that I can get home to you as soon as I can. I am safe and I am sure that I will see you soon.

Dad

I think it has something to do with Fibonacci numbers because he underlined the words "fib" and "sequence". Please help me solve this puzzle so I can get my dad back!

Catherine

For a few moments, none of us said anything. Normally, Justin would have been thrilled at the opportunity to solve a math problem, but now we all sat in stunned silence. This wasn't just a math problem— this was about saving someone's life!

"Where do we start?" I asked. "Does anyone know anything about Fibonacci numbers?"

"I do." Stephanie smiled. "Catherine told me."

Stephanie pulled out the tattered book Catherine had given her and opened it to the page she had bookmarked.

"The Fibonacci sequence was named after an Italian mathematician named Leonardo of Pisa, who was also known as Fibonacci. He wrote about the sequence in a book he wrote in 1202. The first two numbers in the sequence are one and one. You get the next number in the sequence by adding the last two numbers. To get the third number, you add one and one to get two. To get the fourth number, you add one and two to get three. The sequence keeps going like that."

Stephanie wrote down the first few numbers of the Fibonacci sequence on Justin's whiteboard:

1, 1, 2, 3, 5, 8, 13, 21, 34,

We looked at the numbers and then back at the note again. No one said a word as we tried to understand the message Catherine's dad was trying to send to his daughter.

"I think Catherine is right," Justin said. "I think underlining those two words was definitely the first clue. There are other clues there, too, I think. In the second sentence, he says 'I think you'll find where I am.' I think he's telling us that the message is a clue to where he is."

"That's brilliant!" I said.

"I think the first part of the message is telling us how he hid the message. I think he hid his location in the second half of the message," Justin said.

We all looked at the message again:

I am usually at a loss for words when it comes to situations like this, but, in this case, one should cooperate fully and do what they say. I am in the middle of this problem but I'm sure I can find the right solution if I think hard enough. I hate being apart from you and I will fully cooperate with the kidnappers so that I can get home to you as soon as I can. I am safe, and I am sure that I will see you soon.

Dad

"I think you may be right, Justin," Stephanie said. "Look at the first four words. If you take out the word 'usually,' it would say 'I am at.'"

"Maybe the Fibonacci sequence will tell us which words to remove!" I shouted.

For the next half hour, we tried removing words, but nothing seemed to make any sense. We were about to give up when I had an idea.

"What if it's not about which words to remove?" I asked. "What if the Fibonacci sequence is telling us which words to keep?"

We circled the first two words, since the first two numbers in the Fibonacci sequence are 1 and 1. We then counted two words and circled that word, then three and circled that one. We kept circling the words as described by the Fibonacci sequence. When we were done, the note looked like this:

(I)(am) usually (at) a loss (for) words when it comes (to) situations like this, but, in this case, (one) should cooperate fully and do what they say. I am in the (middle) of this problem but I'm sure I can find the right solution if I think hard enough. I hate being (apart) from you and I will fully cooperate with the kidnappers so that I can get home to you as soon as I can. I am safe, and I am sure that I will (see) you soon.

Dad

Stephanie wrote the circled words on the board:

I am at for to one middle apart see.

"Well, it was a good idea, Jordan, but that doesn't make any sense, either," Stephanie said glumly.

"Any ideas, Justin?" I asked.

Justin nodded his head. "Um hmm," he answered,

but he wasn't really responding to my question. He was off in what I called his "zone." He gets so deep in thought that he turns everything else off. When he is in the zone he will answer "um hmm" to anything you say. We waited quietly as he stared at the nonsense sentence Stephanie had written on the board. Finally, he looked up with a large smile.

"They're not words," he said.

"What's not words?" I asked.

"The words in the sentence. They aren't words."

"You lost me," Stephanie said. "What do you mean the words aren't words?"

"The words are numbers. It will be easier if I show you," Justin said as he picked up a marker.

I AM AT FOR TO ONE MIDDLE APART SEE.

Underneath the message, he wrote this:

I AM AT 421 MIDDLE APARTMENT C.

It took Stephanie and me a few seconds to understand, but then it made perfect sense. Catherine's dad had used words that sounded just like numbers, so instead of "for," he really meant the number 4. Instead of "to," he meant the number 2. "Apart" was just an abbreviation for *apartment*. Instead of the word "see," he really meant the letter *C*.

"Oh my gosh," Stephanie said. "We know where the kidnappers are holding Catherine's father!"

CHAPTER 12

W hat do we do now?" I asked.

I had met Stephanie and Justin on the playground before school. We had all told our parents we needed to get in early to practice for the math competition the next day. Little did they know, the math competition was the furthest thing from our minds.

"I think we should go to the FBI and tell them what we know," Stephanie said.

"What if they don't believe us?" I asked. "We're just kids. Do you really think we have a chance of convincing them?"

"Maybe not, but what other choice do we have?"

"We need to gather more evidence," Justin said.

"Are you crazy? You are not talking about going to that apartment, are you?" I asked.

Justin didn't answer, but I could tell by the look on his face that it was exactly what he was thinking. Stephanie began to nervously tug on her ponytail.

The school bell sounded.

"Meet me by the flagpole at noon," Justin said. He then turned and headed away from the school building.

"What about school? Where are you going?" I called after him.

"Just meet me by the flagpole at noon," he called back.

And with that, Justin was gone. Stephanie and I walked slowly into the school, continuing to look back to see if Justin had changed his mind. We had math group that morning, but we didn't even try to solve any of the problems Mrs. Gouche gave us. Our teacher looked at us suspiciously several times but didn't say anything. Instead of working on the problems, Stephanie and I whispered back and forth, trying to figure out what Justin was up to. The morning dragged on with nothing for us to do but worry.

At half past eleven the lunch bell rang, but neither of us felt like eating. We sat in the cafeteria until the crowd of kids made their way out to the playground. Stephanie and I waited until we were the only ones left, then snuck back into the hallway and exited the school through the front entrance. We ran down the walkway until we got to the flagpole in the front circular driveway. We looked around, but Justin was nowhere to be found.

"Now what?" Stephanie asked.

"He'll be here," I said. "Trust me, Justin has a plan."

"That's what I'm worried about." Stephanie's fingers drifted to her ponytail for another nervous tug.

We heard a horn honk and a car pulled into the drive, Justin's mom at the wheel. Justin called from the front seat, "C'mon guys, we're going to be late for practice."

"What is he talking about?" Stephanie asked me quietly.

"Just go with it," I said.

The car was a surprise, but not as big as the one we found in the back seat. Catherine Duchesne was sitting against the window with a bulky backpack on her lap. She had a forced smile on her face. Stephanie and I got in the back seat without saying a word.

"Are you kids excited about the competition?" asked Mrs. Grant.

"Um, sure," I answered.

"I'm just glad we've got one more afternoon to practice and we've got a team to practice against," Justin said.

Stephanie looked sideways at me. I shrugged my shoulders to let her know I had no idea what Justin was talking about.

"Luckily, my mom was available to drive us to the school," Justin continued.

"Yeah, that was lucky alright," I said lamely.

Everyone in the car went silent. Stephanie and I just stared at Catherine and Justin, trying to figure out what was going on. Questions ran through our heads as Mrs. Grant drove through the tree-lined streets. Catherine's face was tense, and she fiddled with the straps on the backpack throughout the ride.

Fifteen minutes later, the car pulled into the Elm Grove Elementary School parking lot. Justin hopped out quickly and we followed his lead.

"Thanks, mom!" he called into the car. Mrs. Grant

waved and pulled back into traffic. We waved back, then turned to Justin as she drove out of sight.

"What is going on?" I asked.

Stephanie had questions of her own. "Where are we? How did you get Catherine out of the house?"

I chimed in with more questions. "What's in the backpack? What are we doing at Elm Grove?"

"Hold on, everybody!" Justin shouted. "I'll answer all your questions, but let's do it while we're walking." With that, he walked quickly onto the sidewalk and away from the school. Despite his short legs, we had to hurry to keep up with him.

"Okay, here's the deal," Justin began. "I had my mom drop us off at Elm Grove because it's only three blocks from Middle Street. My plan is to get proof that Mr. Duchesne is there. Then we can call in the FBI to rescue him."

"How are we going to get proof?" I asked. "We can't just knock on the door and ask for him."

"That's exactly what we're going to do," Justin said.

"Are you crazy?" Stephanie yelled.

"Trust me, I have a plan." Justin smiled and continued walking.

We reached Middle Street and made a right-hand turn. Three buildings down, and there it was: 421 Middle Street. It was an older two-story apartment building set back from the road with a couple of large elm trees partially blocking our view. We walked past the building and came to a small park on the corner of Middle and Twenty-Third Street. We gathered around Justin as he sat down on a bench.

"So, what's your plan?" Stephanie asked.

"It's a little crazy, but brilliant," said Catherine, speaking up for the first time since we got out of the car.

"First things first," said Stephanie, turning to Catherine. "How did you get out of your house?"

"That part was easy," Catherine answered. "Justin just walked up to the front door and knocked. When Justin asked to see me, Agent Carlson said I wasn't available."

"Just like last time," Justin said with a smile. "But this time I was a little more persistent. Five minutes later, I knocked again, and then five minutes after that, and five minutes after that, and five minutes after that."

"But that doesn't explain how Catherine got out," I said.

"Well, by then I knew it was Justin, of course, so I just waited for him to knock again. When the agent went to the front door, I snuck out the back door," she explained.

"But isn't he going to come looking for you?" Stephanie asked.

"Probably, but he won't have any idea where to look, will he?" Catherine grinned.

"Okay, so here's my idea," Justin said. We listened intently as he told us what he wanted to do. At times, we shook our heads and offered minor improvements to the plan, but, in the end, Stephanie and I agreed with Catherine. The plan was a little crazy, but it was brilliant.

Now it was time to see if it would work.

CHAPTER 13

The first part of the plan was easy, but maybe the most dangerous. Justin would knock on the door of apartment C. We weren't sure if the kidnappers would answer the door. If they did, Justin was going to pretend to be selling magazine subscriptions. We did this at our school every year to raise money for playground equipment, school supplies, and stuff like that, so Justin had some old forms he could use as a prop. If someone answered, it would give Justin a chance to take a quick look inside the apartment.

Stephanie and I kept watch on the front of the apartment building. Apartment C was on the second floor. Catherine's job was to keep an eye on the back of the building. There was a sliding glass door leading to a small balcony, but there was a thick curtain covering the door.

When everyone was in position, Justin went into the building. We waited anxiously until he reappeared several minutes later.

"Well? Did you get a look inside?" I asked.

"No luck," he answered. "I knocked a couple times, but no one answered."

"Maybe we didn't get the right apartment," Stephanie said in discouragement, one hand reaching up to take a nervous tug on her ponytail.

"No, I think we've got the right place. I'm pretty sure I heard someone inside," Justin said. "The door has one of those peephole things, so the people inside can see into the hallway."

"What do we do next?" Stephanie asked.

"Well, if they won't let us in, I guess we'll have to get them to come out," Justin said. "It's time for Operation Robbie!"

Stephanie looked confused, but Catherine and I had been in school last year when Robbie had pulled the fire alarm right before our geography test. We explained to Stephanie that the entire school had been evacuated and we weren't allowed back in until the firefighters had examined the building to make sure there wasn't a fire. Mrs. Marks had postponed the geography test until the next day. Robbie had gotten away with it since no one could prove he had done it, but I heard him bragging about it weeks later to the other bullies.

"Everyone knows the plan, right?" Justin asked. "When the fire alarm goes off, the kidnappers will come into the hall to see what's going on. Jordan and I will use our cell phones to take video of their faces. We'll send the video to the FBI and they can use their facial recognition software to identify the kidnappers."

"They're going to be pretty mad if they catch us," I

said worriedly.

"Then let's not get caught," said Justin. "Keep out of sight and take the video through the little window in the door at the end of the hall. I've got rope to tie the door shut so they can't follow us."

He looked down at his phone. "It's 2:11," he said. "Everybody get ready. Stephanie, pull the alarm at exactly 2:15."

Justin and I positioned ourselves at either end of the second-floor hallway. I double-checked the knot on the rope I had used to tie the doorknob to the metal railing on the staircase. My cell phone was out, ready to record the kidnappers bursting out of the apartment.

Catherine was once again watching the back of the building. Stephanie was in the first-floor hallway, ready to pull the fire alarm. I watched anxiously as the time ticked down.

2:12

2:13

2:14

At 2:15 on the dot, Stephanie pulled the alarm!
Nothing happened.

No ear-shattering alarm went off. No sprinkler heads began to spray water from the ceilings. Operation Robbie failed without a sound.

At 2:30, we were all back on the side of the apartment building. Catherine looked very discouraged.

"What now?" she asked.

"We're not done yet," Justin said with determination.

"It's time for Operation Sniffy!"

Stephanie looked confused again, but once again Catherine and I knew just what he was talking about. We explained that last year, Sniffy had received ten days of after-school detention when he set off a string of firecrackers in the hallway.

Justin reached into the backpack and pulled out a book of matches and a package of firecrackers. They were strung together so that you could light one fuse and all fifty firecrackers would explode one after the other, making a noise that sounded like a machine gun.

"They'll have to open the door when they hear these," Justin said.

"But what about the door? You won't be able to tie it closed," I said.

"If they head my way, I guess I'll have to run then, won't I?" he said in a voice that sounded a little shaky.

He was heading toward the front of the building when Stephanie called him back. "Let me do it," she said. "I'm a lot faster than you, so it will be easier for me to get away."

Stephanie had a good point. Justin wasn't exactly the fastest runner. Stephanie had been playing soccer since she was three years old and was the fastest kid in our class. She was even faster than Robbie, who was a pretty good athlete himself.

"Okay, you light the firecrackers and I'll record video from the end of the hallway. That will give me more time to run if they come my way," Justin said.

He reached into his backpack and pulled out a roll of duct tape. He tore off a strip about four inches long and handed it to Stephanie.

"What's this for?" she asked.

"Before you light the fuse, cover up the peephole so they can't look outside," Justin answered. "The only way they'll be able to find out what's going on is to open the door."

"That's brilliant!" she said in admiration.

"Okay, wait five minutes for everyone else get in place," Justin said. "I'll give you the signal."

Justin and I positioned ourselves at each end of the second-floor hallway again with our cell phones ready to go. I checked my knot for what seemed like the tenth time. It felt secure. I stood in front of the window with my cell phone ready to record.

Justin was at the other end of the hall, his phone out and ready. When he gave the signal, Stephanie placed the duct tape over the peephole and lit the fuse.

Pop! Pop! Pop! Pop! The firecrackers began to blast, faster and faster. Stephanie ran for the stairway, racing past Justin on the way down the stairs. The door to apartment C burst open, and a large man in a sweatshirt stumbled into the hallway. I clicked record on my phone but had only recorded a few seconds of video when the man turned toward me. I took off down the stairs. I heard footsteps pounding down the hall and the hallway door slam against the wall. My rope hadn't even slowed him down.

I took the stairs two at a time. I had a moment of panic when I couldn't get the outside door open, then realized I was trying to pull when I needed to push. I could hear heavy footsteps coming quickly down the stairs behind me when I pushed the door open and stumbled out onto the walkway in front of the building. Without looking back, I ran as fast as I could.

Justin emerged from the other end of the apartment building, followed closely by a short, stocky man who gained on him with every step. I had my own problems. The large man was only twenty feet behind me now. I could hear his heavy steps getting closer. He would catch me before I got to the street. I zigged to the left to try to put one of the large elm trees between me and the kidnapper. I felt his hand brush over the back of my shirt and put on an extra burst of speed. Just then, Stephanie stepped out from behind the tree and shot something from a spray can into the kidnapper's face. Temporarily blinded, he tripped over a large tree root and fell heavily to the ground.

"What was that?" I shouted to Stephanie.

"Super String!" she shouted back. "Now run!"

She pulled away from me as I looked back at the man behind me. He had staggered to his feet and was peeling the gooey string from his face. We only had a few more steps to run before we would hit the relative safety of the street, when I heard Justin cry out. The stocky man had him by one arm and had lifted him off the ground. Justin's legs were still running, but he wasn't going anywhere.

I came to a stop.

"Run, Jordan!" Stephanie called back to me, but I just couldn't leave my best friend behind. I marched over to the man who was holding Justin.

"Leave him alone!" I shouted, my voice sounding

much braver than I felt.

"What are you little punks playing at?" said the stocky man as the one who had been chasing me came up behind me and pulled my arms roughly behind my back.

"We were just fooling around," Justin said.

"Yeah? Well, I don't like kids, so you better stay away from my apartment!" the taller man said.

"Yes, sir," Justin said meekly.

The two men released us and the larger one pushed me toward the street.

"I don't want to see you around here again!" he said menacingly.

As Justin turned to walk away, his cell phone fell out of his hand, landing with a thump on the grass.

"What's that?" the shorter man asked.

"It's just my phone," said Justin, picking it up from the ground.

"Let me see it," the man said. He grabbed the phone from Justin's hand and noticed it was still recording video. "Taking video of us, huh?"

He dropped the phone to the sidewalk and brought a large booted foot down on it, smashing the phone's screen. Two stomps later, the phone was shattered beyond repair.

"Check that kid, too," he said.

The taller man grabbed the phone from my hand and threw it to the ground. Within seconds, it was also destroyed.

"Now, get out of here!" he shouted. "If I see you kids again, I'll break your heads."

Justin and I did not need a second warning. We took off running as fast as we could. For the first time in his life, Justin actually ran faster than me.

We ran all the way to the park at the end of the street. We were glad to see Stephanie sitting safely on one of the park benches, but our hearts fell when we saw a man in a rumpled gray suit holding Catherine with a tight grip!

CHAPTER 14

L et her go!" I yelled, advancing toward the man holding Catherine.

To my surprise, Catherine laughed.

"Jordan, this is my dad," she said, putting an arm around him.

"Your dad? But I thought—"

Catherine and Stephanie both laughed at the look on my face.

Catherine said, "I'll explain everything later, but right now I suggest we get on the phone to the FBI and let them know my dad is safe."

"And that they've got some kidnappers to pick up," Justin added.

Mr. Duchesne borrowed Stephanie's phone and made the call. After a short while, sirens blared in the distance, and we watched from the safety of the park as several police cars and a SWAT team van pulled up in front of the apartment building. The smaller kidnapper tried to escape out the front door but ran right into the arms of two police officers. A short time later, the second kidnapper was led from the building with his wrists handcuffed behind his back. Both men were put into the back of one of the police cars, which sped away with its lights flashing and siren screaming.

A black car pulled up to the curb in front of the park and Agent Carlson stepped out. He looked happy to see Mr. Duchesne was safe but frowned when he saw Catherine and Justin.

"You know that we were keeping you in the house for your own safety, don't you?" he said sternly to Catherine.

"Yes, sir," she replied with her eyes lowered to the ground.

"And you, young man," he said to Justin. "Do you know it's a crime to interfere with an FBI investigation?"

Justin's eyes widened.

"But in this case, I guess I can let you both off the hook," he said with a smile. "You did, after all, find the clue that Mr. Duchesne left and then came up with a plan to get him out safely."

"And just how did that happen?" I asked, still confused about what had gone on after the firecrackers started to explode.

"Well, I know it wasn't part of the plan, but I thought back to how Justin had gotten me out of my house," said Catherine. "When the agent opened the front door, I went out the back. Only in this case, while the kidnappers chased you and Justin out the front door, I snuck into the building from the back. The apartment was unlocked, so I went in and found my dad tied to a chair."

"Are you crazy?" Stephanie asked. "What if there had been another kidnapper?"

"I guess the plan wouldn't have worked then, would it?" Catherine laughed.

"Catherine cut me free and we made it out the back door before the kidnappers got back," said Mr. Duchesne. "It probably took them a few minutes to find out I was gone because Catherine locked the apartment door behind us."

"That was brilliant," I told Catherine.

"And brave," added Stephanie.

"Those kidnappers are really going to be mad when they realize they were beaten by a bunch of kids," Justin said. "And it's all thanks to you, Catherine."

"I couldn't have done it without all of you, though," Catherine said. "You figured out my dad's note, Justin."

"But it was Jordan who figured out which words in the note we needed to use," Justin pointed out.

"Which I couldn't have done without you letting us know that we needed to use Fibonacci sequence, Catherine," I added.

"And Stephanie lit the firecrackers that got the kidnappers out of the apartment," Catherine said.

"But it was Justin's great idea to bring them," Stephanie said.

"And Jordan came back to rescue me when the kidnapper grabbed me," Justin said.

We all looked at each other and laughed.

"You all make a great team," said Mr. Duchesne.

"Speaking of teams, did you know Catherine joined our math team for the fourth-grade competition tomorrow?" Stephanie asked Mr. Duchesne.

"I didn't know that." Mr. Duchesne looked thoughtfully at Catherine. "But if you kids can do math as well as you solve mysteries, I'd say you have a pretty good team," he said as he gave his daughter another hug.

"So, I can go?" Catherine asked.

"Only under one condition," he said.

We all looked at him in anticipation.

"You'd better win!"

CHAPTER 15

I was so excited about the math competition that I could barely finish my breakfast. The competition was at eleven o'clock, but Catherine and Stephanie were already at the school when Justin and I arrived at half past nine.

"We were getting worried about you guys," Stephanie said, teasing.

"It's not my fault. My alarm didn't go off this morning," Justin said, pulling his smashed cell phone out of his pocket.

We all laughed.

"Why are you keeping that thing?" I asked.

"It's my good luck charm," Justin replied. "It helped us to scare away the burglars from Stephanie's house and now it has helped us rescue Catherine's dad from the kidnappers."

"I guess that's true," I said, wondering if it was too late to retrieve my own broken phone from the trash can. My parents had promised to get me a new one when we explained what had happened.

There wasn't anything more we could do to prepare for the competition, so we spent the next hour just being kids: seeing who could jump the farthest from the swing set, playing a spirited game of tag, and climbing on the monkey bars.

At half past ten, Stephanie said, "So, are we ready to do this?"

"Before we go in," Catherine said softly, "I want you to know how much—" but she couldn't go on as her words were replaced by quiet sobs.

No one said anything for a few long moments while Catherine composed herself.

"I guess I just don't know how to thank you," she said.

"You come up with some answers today and we'll call it even," I said. "Deal?"

"It's a deal," she said with a laugh.

"Hands together," I said. We put our hands together. "Math Kids on three."

"One, two, three, Math Kids!" we shouted in unison.

As we walked into the school, I realized that it really didn't matter if we won the competition. All four of us were already winners just knowing that we had such great friends.

That thought faded as soon as we found Joe Christian waiting for us.

"I'm surprised you even bothered to show up," he said sarcastically. "I'm going to wipe the floor with you guys today."

"Yeah? Where's your team?" Stephanie responded.

"Who cares? I don't need 'em," Joe said in a conceited tone.

"Where's that Super String when I really need it?" Stephanie whispered to me. I laughed.

"Go ahead and laugh all you want," Joe said. "We'll see who's laughing when I'm holding the trophy!" With that, he stamped away.

"I guess he's never heard there's no I in team," Justin said as he watched Joe walk away down the hallway.

"Let's go win this thing, Math Kids," I said with determination.

The math competition had three rounds. The first was individual problem-solving. We figured Joe would do very well in that round. The second round was the team problem-solving round. The top two teams would then compete against each other in the lightning round.

We were in second place coming out of the individual problem-solving round of the competition. We had had thirty minutes to solve as many short problems as we could. The Math Kids got thirty correct. We fist-bumped each other because we knew that would be tough to beat. Joe's teammates only got sixteen right, but Joe got an amazing twenty-four, giving them a total of forty correct answers.

Joe had a wide smile on his face when the first-round scores were announced.

"I told you so," he said to me as he walked past. "Your team is going down."

In the team problem-solving round, we would have another thirty minutes to solve five problems. These problems were much tougher, so each one was worth ten points. A sheet of problems was placed face down in front of each team. At the signal from Coach Harder,

the moderator, we all turned our sheets over quickly.
The clock was ticking.

We quickly read through the five problems:

1. In a 500-page book, the page number is printed
   at the bottom of each page. How many times
   does the number 1 appear?

2. The product of two numbers is 10,000. If neither
   of the numbers contains a 0, what are the two
   numbers?

3. When the order of the digits of 2,552 is reversed,
   the number is the same. How many counting
   numbers between 100 and 1000 are the same
   when the order of their digits is reversed?

4. In the addition problem below, each letter
   represents a digit. What four-digit number does
   DEER represent?

$$
\begin{array}{cccc}
  &   & I & N \\
+ & R & I & D \\
\hline
D & E & E & R \\
\end{array}
$$

5. To write the numbers from 12 to 14, we will
   write a total of six digits (1 2 1 3 1 4). How many
   digits will it take to write the numbers from 1 to
   150?

We had talked before the competition about how to work together in the team problem-solving round. There were a few ways we could go; We could each solve a different problem, and then whoever finished their problem first could start on the last problem. Or, we could work on each problem as a team. We had tried both these methods during our math group practice. What we had figured out is that we were best when we divided into two groups of two. That way, no one would get stuck on a problem by themselves, and we would have a second person to check to make sure the answer was correct.

"Catherine and I will take the first two," said Stephanie.

"That leaves problems three and four for us," I said to Justin.

"We'll meet you at problem five," Justin said. And the race was on!

As it turned out, we all finished at almost the same time, so we all got to work on the last problem together. It was a perfect team problem, so we finished it quickly. We looked at the clock. We had finished all five problems and still had five minutes to go. We saw Joe glance up from his paper and check the time nervously. The three other members of his team had their heads down working, but it was clear they weren't working together as a team.

"Time!" shouted Coach Harder.

We waited while the judges checked the answers for each team. Mrs. Robinson's class had three right, while the team from Mr. Kinney's class only managed two. When they wrote up the score for Joe's team, they wrote a big 40 on the board. His team had only gotten four right! If we had a perfect score on the team problem-solving, we'd get fifty points and we'd be tied!

The judges bent over the table, checking our answers while we waited anxiously. Coach Harder picked up the blue marker and stood in front of the board. He wrote our score and then stepped aside so everyone could see. A perfect fifty! We were tied with Joe's team!

It was all going to come down to the lightning round. It was the Math Kids versus Joe's team. Each team had eighty points, so no one had an advantage going into the round.

"Okay, teams, if you can take your place at your tables, we'll start the final round of the competition," said Coach Harder into his microphone. "During this round, each correct answer will be worth five points. After I've finished reading the question, ring your bell when you have an answer. If your answer is correct, you'll be awarded five points. If not, the other team will be allowed to answer. The round will last for ten minutes. If the two teams are still tied at the end of the round, we will go into sudden death. Does everyone understand the rules?"

Both teams nodded.

"Are both teams ready to start?"

We nodded nervously. Joe, on the other hand, looked supremely confident.

"Start the clock. Here is the first question. I have forty socks in a drawer: twelve tan, nine brown, eleven gray, and eight blue. It is pitch black. How many socks do I need to pull out to guarantee I have a matching pair?"

Stephanie slammed her hand on the bell.

"Five," she said.

"Correct!" said Coach Harder.

Stephanie winked at Catherine and mouthed "thanks" to her.

"What is the smallest whole number that uses the letter *a* in its English spelling?" asked Coach Harder.

Joe hit the bell as he yelled out, "One thousand!"

"That's correct."

The score was tied again. And on it went throughout the round. We'd get one right, then Joe would answer one. Sometimes Joe was on top; sometimes we were in the lead. As the time ticked down for the round, no one could manage to pull ahead. The round ended with both teams still tied.

"Since both teams are still tied, we'll now go into sudden death. The first team to get a correct answer will be our winner," said Coach Harder. "Are both teams ready?"

We nodded nervously. Joe didn't look as confident as he had when the lightning round started. Coach Harder pulled the next question card, looked at both teams, and then read, "What is the tenth number in the sequence of Fibonacci numbers?"

Catherine's hand hit the bell in a flash. At the sound of the bell, Joe looked up in shock.

"The answer is fifty-five," Catherine said confidently.

"That is correct, and the Math Kids are the winners!" Coach Harder said with a smile.

We swarmed around Catherine, hugging her and patting her on the back.

"How did you know that?" I asked in amazement.

"Maybe you haven't noticed, but fifty-five is my favorite number," Catherine said.

"It's our favorite number now, too," I said.

CHAPTER 16

We were still celebrating on Monday morning as the four Math Kids walked to school. Justin high-fived me about every twenty steps. My hand was starting to get sore by the time we reached the playground, but I didn't care. There wasn't anything that was going to ruin my good mood today.

How wrong that thought turned out to be. In the next twenty minutes, my day went from fantastic to absolutely horrible.

It started when we ran into the bullies waiting in the hallway outside our classroom.

"Just because you nerds won some stupid contest doesn't mean we won't be waiting for you after school today," Robbie said threateningly.

"Yeah," chimed in Sniffy.

"We're not afraid of you," said Catherine, although I wanted to tell her to speak for herself, because I was certainly afraid of them.

"We'll see about that after school," said Robbie.

"Yeah," said Sniffy.

We ducked into the classroom before things could get worse, but it wasn't any better in there, either. Mrs. McDonald was standing in front of Mrs. Gouche's desk, her finger bobbing up and down as she yelled at our teacher.

"Someone is responsible for tricking my daughter, and a lot of other kids, too, I might add, into showing up for a singing competition that never happened!" yelled Mrs. McDonald.

"But I don't know anything about it," said Mrs. Gouche. "I saw the flyers, but I don't know who put them up."

"Well, somebody knows, and I'm going to find out who!" Mrs. McDonald shouted as she stormed out of the room.

I had almost forgotten about our trick to get Susie off our team. Mrs. McDonald was like a dog with a bone. She wasn't going to just let this thing go. So now I had that *and* the bullies to worry about. *Could anything else go wrong today?*

Unfortunately, the answer was yes. Our math team was called to the principal's office after lunch. Mrs. Arnold didn't waste any time in getting to the reason for us being there.

"Joe Christian believes that your team cheated in the math competition this weekend," she said.

"What?" I asked in amazement.

"He thinks you knew the questions ahead of time," she answered. "He and his parents will arrive soon to discuss this, but I wanted to give you a chance to explain before they get here."

"There's nothing to explain," Justin said. Catherine, Stephanie, and I nodded strongly in agreement.

"Okay, please wait by the secretary's desk until I call for you," she said sternly.

"This day went from great to lousy pretty quick, didn't it?" I said when we plopped down onto the chairs.

"Does anyone know what she's talking about?" asked Stephanie. "We won fair and square."

We didn't have long to wait. Joe Christian and his parents entered the office about ten minutes later. The secretary showed them into the principal's office. After a short time, we were asked to join them.

"Joe believes that the math competition might not have been fair," Mrs. Arnold started.

"What wasn't fair?" I asked.

"There's no way you could have come up with that last answer so quickly without knowing what the question was ahead of time," Joe accused, pointing his finger at Catherine. "How many other questions did you know about?"

Catherine responded by laughing. Everyone looked at her in amazement, including Stephanie, Justin, and me.

"You think I didn't know that fifty-five is the tenth number in the Fibonacci series?" she asked Joe.

"No, I don't," he said stubbornly. "No one knows that off the top of their head."

"Oh yeah? Well, what if I told you I do know that off the top of my head? Let me tell you a few other things about the number fifty-five," she said. "Fifty-five is also a triangular number. It's the sum of the first ten numbers."

Everyone in the room was now looking at Catherine, but she was just getting started.

"In fact, fifty-five happens to be the largest Fibonacci number that is also a triangular number," she added. "It's also the sum of the squares of the first five numbers. You want more? The number fifty-five is also a Kaprekar number. If you multiply it by itself, you get 3025, and thirty plus twenty-five equals fifty-five."

The room grew silent. Stephanie, Justin, and I tried to suppress the smiles on our faces, but we weren't very successful. Mrs. Arnold was also smiling a little. She looked over at Joe's parents.

"It sounds like Catherine knows quite a bit about the number fifty-five," she said. "Were there any other questions you thought were unfair?"

Joe's parents looked at each other and then at Joe, who was taking a sudden interest in his shoes.

"No, I think her explanation was good enough for me," Mr. Christian said. "Good enough for you, son?"

Joe mumbled a few words under his breath.

"I'm sorry, I didn't hear you, Joe," Mrs. Arnold said.

"Yeah, that's good," Joe said, a little louder this time.

Joe and his parents rose. His parents thanked the principal for her time and left quickly. Mrs. Arnold smiled broadly after they were gone.

"That's very impressive, Catherine," Mrs. Arnold said.

"Well, it is my favorite number," Catherine said with pride.

"I can tell," the principal responded.

I rose to return to class.

"Not so fast, Jordan," said Mrs. Arnold, the smile now gone from her face.

"Yes, ma'am?"

"There's the other matter of a singing contest. You wouldn't know anything about that, would you?"

The look on my face was all the confession she needed.

"And the rest of you were in on this, too?" Mrs. Arnold asked.

"Catherine didn't know," Stephanie said. "It was all our idea. We wanted her to be on our team instead of Susie."

"Do you know how upset Susie is? Did you even consider that?" asked Mrs. Arnold.

We all looked down, feeling ashamed of how we had fooled Susie. Mrs. Arnold let us suffer for a long moment, then burst into laughter.

"I wish I could have seen the look on her face," she said.

When we began to laugh, she silenced us with a stern look.

"And I'll deny ever saying that. Now get back to class!" she said.

On the way back to class, I felt very relieved, but I knew we weren't out of the woods yet.

"Two problems down, and one to go," I said. We still had the bullies waiting on us at the end of the day.

"I'm not worried about them," Catherine said defiantly. I wished I had her confidence.

At the end of the day, we followed Catherine out to the playground. As they had promised, the bullies were there. Robbie, Sniffy, Bill, and Bryce stood in a line blocking our path.

"Well, nerds, what now?" said Robbie.

"You tell us—you're the ones in our way," Catherine replied.

"We got detention for that little stunt you pulled with the spitball," Bill said.

"Yeah," said Sniffy, adding nothing to the conversation as usual.

"So?" Stephanie challenged.

"So, you're going to pay for it," Robbie said.

"We weren't afraid of kidnappers, so why should we be afraid of you?" Catherine said firmly.

Robbie's face began to turn red. He clenched his fists at his sides. He moved toward Catherine, but Stephanie, Justin, and I stepped in front of her. Sniffy, Bill, and Bryce were on the move, too, surrounding us on all sides.

"FBI! Everybody freeze!" came a loud voice from the edge of the playground.

Everybody froze in place, but our heads all turned toward the voice. I was shocked to see Special Agent Carlson walking toward us with his FBI credentials held out in front of him.

"You four, over here!" he barked to the Math Kids.

Then he turned to the four bullies. For a long moment, he didn't say a word—just examined them with a disgusted look on his face.

"What do you have to say for yourself?" he asked Robbie.

Robbie stammered, trying to get out a couple words, but finally said they weren't doing anything wrong.

"Is that right, Robert?" Agent Carlson asked.

Robbie looked surprised that the FBI agent knew his name. That look of surprise turned to one of shock at the agent's next question.

"Are you aware of the penalty for pulling a fire alarm, young man?"

Robbie's face went white. "Please, whatever you do, please don't tell my dad," he pleaded.

The agent gave Robbie a long look, but he wasn't done yet. He turned his attention to Sniffy.

"As for you, Brian, I'm sure you know it is a felony to set off explosive devices inside a school building, don't you?"

Sniffy didn't say anything—just stared down at the ground. He gave a big sniff as he tried to hold back tears.

"I'm going to give you a break today, kids. I'm not going to recommend prosecution of these serious offenses—yet." The agent paused to let the seriousness of his words sink in. "But if I hear one word from my juvenile undercover team that you are threatening anyone at this school, I'll be happy to bring in my team to make arrests. Is that understood?"

The bullies nodded.

"I said, is that understood?" the agent asked again firmly.

The boys responded in a loud chorus, "Yes sir."

"Good. Now get out of here!" Agent Carlson boomed. The boys scattered, running from the playground as fast as their legs could carry them.

Special Agent Carlson turned to us with a smile.

"Do you really have a juvenile undercover team?" Justin asked in awe.

"I do now," he replied.

"We're going to be part of the FBI?" I asked.

"Not officially, but those bullies don't need to know that, do they?" he answered. "And, unofficially, I could use your help on an ongoing case I have."

"Are you serious?" Justin asked.

"Totally serious. One of the clues looks like it involves some math that I think you might be able to help me with," the agent said. "If you are up to the challenge, that is."

"I think I can speak for all of us, Agent Carlson," I said, looking at Justin, Stephanie, and Catherine for acknowledgement. "We're in!"

"Great. Come down to the FBI office tomorrow after school and I'll go over the case with you," he said. "By the way, how did your math contest go?" Special Agent Carlson asked, although I had a strong feeling he already knew the answer.

"We won!" Catherine yelled.

"Good job. Oh, that reminds me, I have something for all of you."

We followed him to his car, where he pulled a cardboard box from his trunk. He opened the box and pulled out four jerseys. They were red and black, matching our school colors. Each jersey had *Math Kids* printed across the front and each of our names on the back, curving over the jersey number.

Catherine's jersey number was 55, of course.

THE END

COMING FALL 2019! AN UNUSUAL PATTERN, BOOK 3 IN THE MATH KIDS SERIES. DON'T MISS IT!

THE MATH KIDS ARE AT IT AGAIN! WHEN THEIR NEW FRIEND, SPECIAL AGENT CARLSON, ASKS THEM TO LOOK AT A CRYPTIC POEM WRITTEN BY A DYING BANK ROBBER, THEY KNOW THEY WILL NEED ALL OF THEIR MATH SKILLS TO CRACK THE CASE.

THE POEM ISN'T THEIR ONLY PROBLEM, THOUGH. THEIR FAVORITE SCHOOL JANITOR IS FIRED FOR STEALING FROM STUDENTS' LOCKERS. THE MATH KIDS KNOW OLD MIKE WOULD NEVER DO ANYTHING LIKE THAT, BUT HOW CAN THEY PROVE IT, ESPECIALLY WITH THE NEW JANITOR WATCHING THEIR EVERY MOVE?

JORDAN, STEPHANIE, JUSTIN, AND CATHERINE WILL NEED MATH, BRAVERY, AND A LITTLE BIT OF LUCK IF THEY HOPE TO SOLVE THE BANK ROBBERY CASE AND GET OLD MIKE HIS JOB BACK. WILL THEY BE ABLE TO FIGURE OUT THE UNUSUAL PATTERN IN TIME?

APPENDIX

FACTORIALS

Factorials are used to find the number of ways we can order elements in a set. For example, how many ways can we arrange the numbers in the set {1, 2, 3}?

$$1, 2, 3$$
$$1, 3, 2$$
$$2, 1, 3$$
$$2, 3, 1$$
$$3, 1, 2$$
$$3, 2, 1$$

For three elements in a set, there are six different ways we can arrange them. We can show this using the equation $3! = 6$.

A factorial is written by putting an exclamation point after the number. To calculate a factorial, we just multiply all the numbers from 1 to the number:

$$3! = 3 \times 2 \times 1 = 6$$
$$4! = 4 \times 3 \times 2 \times 1 = 24$$
$$5! = 5 \times 4 \times 3 \times 2 \times 1 = 120$$

Factorials get big really fast. For example, 5! = 120 but 10! = 3,628,800.

There is one tricky thing about factorials. You would probably think that 0! would be equal to 0, but it's actually equal to 1. One reason for this is that there is only one way to arrange a set with no elements.

So just memorize this one: 0! = 1.

It was this tricky part of factorials that Catherine knew, which allowed Justin to solve The Sixes Problem for the number 0.

$$(0! + 0! + 0!)! = (1 + 1 + 1)! = 3! = 3 \times 2 \times 1 = 6$$

PIGEONHOLE PRINCIPLE

Imagine there is a big storm and 10 pigeons try to get

out of the rain. If there are only 9 holes, at least 1 hole will have 2 pigeons in it.

The pigeonhole principle—sometimes called Dirichlet's Box Principle after the mathematician Peter Gustav Lejeune Dirichlet—seems very simple, but it is really very powerful.

There is another version of the pigeonhole principle that says the biggest number in a group must be at least as big as the average number. Let's say we have 5 pigeons and only 2 pigeonholes. The average number of pigeons in a hole is 5 divided by 2, or 2½. Since the biggest number of pigeons in a hole must be at least 2½, that means that there must be at least 3 pigeons in 1 hole, since we can't have half of a pigeon in a hole.

Here's another example of how we can use this principle: If there are 6,000 American students at a college, at least 120 of them must be from the same state. How do we know? The average number of students from each state is 6,000 ÷ 50 = 120. The pigeonhole principle then tells us there must be at least 120 from the same state since the maximum number of students from one state must be at least as large as the average.

MENTAL MATH

Mental math is math you can do in your head. It can amaze your friends and can even make doing your homework easier. Catherine taught her friends to multiply two-digit numbers in their heads.

Here are the rules that make it work:

- Both numbers must be two digits.
- The first digit (the tens digit) must be the same for both numbers.
- The last digit (the ones digit) of each number

must add up to 10.

Let's try this for 45 × 45. We can do this because the tens digit is 4 for both numbers and the ones digits add up to 10.

To get the first two digits of the answer, multiply the tens digit by one more than the tens digit. The tens digit is 4, so we want to multiply 4 × 5 (because 5 is one more than 4):

$$4 \times 5 = 20$$

To get the last two digits of the answer, just multiply the ones digits together:

$$5 \times 5 = 25$$

Put all four digits together and we get the answer of 2,025.

There is one more thing you need to know. If the two ones digits are 1 and 9, we only get 9 when we multiply them together. Since these are the last two digits of the answer, we'll show this as 09 in our answer. For example, 31 × 39 = 1,209.

CONTEST ANSWERS

1) In a 500-page book, the page number is printed at the bottom of each page. How many times does the number 1 appear?

Hints that will help you solve this problem:

- In the first 100 pages, how many pages have the number 1?
- Is it the same for the next 100 pages?
- Is there anything different about the pages 100–199?

Answer: 200

2) The product of two numbers is 10,000. If neither of the numbers contains a 0, what are the two numbers?

Hints that will help you solve this problem:

- If we multiply two numbers and get a 0 in the ones digit, one of the two numbers must end in 5 and the other must end in 2, 4, 6, or 8 (since $2 \times 5 = 10$, $4 \times 5 = 20$, $6 \times 5 = 30$, and $8 \times 5 = 40$).
- Try dividing 10,000 by different numbers ending in 5 to narrow down the choices.

Answer: 16 and 625

3) When the order of the digits of 2,552 is reversed, the number is the same. How many counting numbers between 100 and 1000 are the same when the order of their digits is reversed?

Hints that will help you solve this problem:

- How many reversible numbers are there between 100 and 200?
- How many reversible numbers are there between 200 and 300?

Do you see a pattern?

Answer: 90

4) In the addition problem below, each letter represents a digit. What four-digit number does DEER represent?

```
      I N
+   R I D
  ───────
  D E E R
```

Hints that will help you solve this problem:

D must be equal to 1 since it is carried.
R must be equal to 9 since we know it carries over.
N must be equal to 8 since N + 1 = 9.

Answer: DEER = 1,009

The whole equation is

```
        5 8
+     9 5 1
  ─────────
  1 0 0 9
```

5) To write the numbers from 12 to 14, we will write a total of six digits (1 2 1 3 1 4). How many digits will it take to write the numbers from 1 to 150?

Hints that will help you solve this problem:

How many one-digit numbers are there?
How many two-digit numbers are there?
How many three-digit numbers are there?

Answer: 342 digits

ACKNOWLEDGMENTS

The whole team at Common Deer Press continues to amaze me with their dedication and professionalism, all while being the most supportive team on the planet. Thanks, team!

There aren't enough accolades I can give to Kirsten Marion. The characters in these books seem to come alive under your brilliant and insightful guidance. I think you know Stephanie and the rest of the kids even better than I do.

Thanks to Heather Kohlmann, for making sure all my t's were crossed and my i's dotted. Your attention to detail is amazing!

Once again, Shannon O'Toole's beautiful artwork blew me away, bringing words to life in a way only she can.

In a conversation over lunch one day, I mentioned my writing aspirations to Jeremy Rodriguez, a work colleague. He encouraged me to try to publish these books, even providing me with a primer on book publishing. The seed he planted grew into The Math Kids series. These books would be just ones and zeros on a dusty hard drive somewhere without his inspiration.

To my son Jordan, who always has a hug for me every morning—you'll never know how much those hugs mean.

As a parent, you want your kids to be happy and successful, but also for them to treat other people well and to make the world a better place. If I'm graded for my kids someday, I feel pretty good about the A+ I am going to receive.

Finally, for my wife—who is ecstatic that I've found a hobby that doesn't cost her any money—thanks for always listening, even when I'm just venting (especially when I'm just venting).

ABOUT THE AUTHOR

*D*avid Cole has been interested in math since was very young. He pursued degrees in math and computer science. He has shared this love of math at many levels, including teaching at the college level and coaching elementary math teams. He also ran a summer math camp for a number of years. He has always loved to write and penned a number of plays which have found their way on stage. David had always wanted to combine his love of math and writing, and now with The Math Kids, he has done just that! He feels that writing about math is a great way to exercise both sides of the brain at the same time.

In case you haven't already, catch the beginning of this adventure by reading *The Math Kids: The Prime-Time Burglars.*